"*Quare Hawks* is a collision
between old and new Ireland.
Both heartbreaking and hilarious,
and hopeful and despairing.
Eddie Stack has a way of making
you laugh and cry at the same time.
A brilliant collection
from a great Irish storyteller."

Willy Vlautin,
author of
Lean on Pete, Motel Life
and Northline

Bobogue: winner of the 2009 Caomhnú Award for fiction; first published in *The South Circular*, March 2012.

Blue Money: first published in *Crannog*, summer 2009

It Couldn't Have Happened to a Nicer Man: first published in *Southwords*, summer 2011

Mr. Jones: winner of Irish Writing Center's *Lonely Voices*, January 2010

•

Quare Hawks was first published by Tintaun for Amazon Kindle in August 2012

This paperback edition published by Tintaun in January 2013

•

ISBN 978-1-930579-00-2

Design + Layout: Bill Roarty
Cover image: Phillip Morrison (www.PhillipMorrison.com)
Back Cover Portrait: Anthony Holdsworth (www.AnthonyHoldsworth.com)

Tintaun Media
Galway & San Francisco

Quare Hawks

Stories by

Eddie Stack

CONTENTS

BOBOGUE

THE LOCALS WERE WARY OF BOBOGUE. CHILDREN WHISPERED THAT she was a witch; adults said she was odd, that there was a stain in her blood. Thirty years old or maybe more, she'd never had a job and drew Social Welfare as an unemployed poet. She lived a few miles outside town, on a small dysfunctional farm with her brother Paddy, another unemployed poet.

Twice a week, Bobogue traveled to town on an old red Vespa. In custard-coloured sailing jacket, wild black hair blowing in the wind, she took her time, often halting to smell flowers, pick berries or talk to a horse in a field. The Vespa was seldom road-legal, so she parked it out of harm's way, in Duffy's Lane at the edge of town. From there she walked to Maguire's Supermarket, the post-office, the dole office, the newsagents. If it rained — and she didn't understand why she did this — she browsed in the chemist's shop, soaking up the smells and reading the instructions on medicine packages. But never bought anything. Last call before heading home was Harbour Hotel for a cup of coffee, two cigarettes and a view of the sea. On the return journey she counted the words she'd spoken during the expedition, like they were spent coins. A dozen was average, but once she did it in seven, which was a record. If a trip involved conversation of any length, she didn't bother counting the words, but that seldom happened.

The weather was unseasonably warm for May—'pet-weather,' the old people called it. Bobogue sipped coffee in the hotel bar and watched the early summer activity—a sailing boat maneuvering in the harbour, children fishing from the pier, three orange kayaks being launched on the slipway.

Jason Berry watched her from the counter while he sipped gin and tonic. As if feeling his eyes on her, Bobogue slowly turned and squinted at him: a stranger. Jason thought she was smiling and flashed a grin. She turned away and looked out the window, one eye on his reflection in the glass.

A few weeks afterwards, they met in Maguire's Supermarket. Bobogue was picking up a few cans of Guinness for her brother when Jason docked beside her and said, "Hello." She nodded.

"Know much about wine?" he asked.

She shook her head and moved away.

Later he saw her biking home and saluted her. Bobogue glanced back, puzzled. After that, he scanned the streets for her whenever he was passing. Once, driving through with his wife, he saw her outside the post office and almost honked.

June twelfth was Bobogue's birthday and she celebrated with an Irish coffee in the Harbour Hotel. She looked out the sea-view window, lit a cigarette and got lost in a tangle of thoughts about age and death. Jason watched her from the counter. Finally he took his drink to a neighbouring table and said,

"Hello there, enjoying the view?"

"Yeah."

"Beautiful around here."

"Yeah."

"You're local, right?"

She nodded and sipped her drink. A waiter left another one beside her.

"It's on me," Jason said.

"Thanks."

"You're welcome. I'm Jason."

He offered his hand and she shook it meekly, blushing a smile.

"I'm Bobogue."

"Nice to meet you, Bobogue. What a lovely name. What does it mean?"

"Just a name," she shrugged.

Jason moved to her table. Fair and fit, with bronzed face and expensive watch, he looked like a model in a Sunday magazine. She lit another cigarette. He praised the beauty of the countryside, the friendliness of the people. Then he asked,

"What do you do?"

"Write poetry."

"Really? I thought there was something different about you. I'm in IT. Computers. Software."

She nodded.

"Have you any poems published?"

Bobogue shook her head, tapped ash from her cigarette and inhaled deeply. A line of poetry came to her and she smiled and felt a little light-headed when Jason called another round. The third drink had her humming and the world lit up. Words began to flutter like butterflies in her heart and she said,

"You've made my birthday."

After two more Irish coffees, Bobogue was sitting in the passenger's seat of Jason's white Volvo, sunroof open, stereo playing the Waterboys. She directed him through the narrow roads of the peninsula, her head bobbing to the songs. Bobogue navigated him to a cul-de-sac, near a monument to the ill-fated Spanish Armada. They crossed the sand dunes to a small beach and Bobogue ran to the water, threw off her clothes, and waded naked into the waves. Jason muttered 'Jesus,' and sat on a black rock.

They made love in a grassy hollow above the beach and it was a fast act. Bobogue was naked and Jason's pants were at his knees. He turned away from her almost immediately and when she tried to caress him into giving more he said, "We'd better go, I've things to do."

Five times in two weeks they made love in that same place. She'd park the Vespa in Duffy's Lane and wait in the hotel until he arrived. Her brother Paddy noticed she spent more time away. She had become almost loquacious and sang self-penned love songs when she was at home.

Jason became elusive and her mood changed. She occasionally

caught glimpses of him or his car, but could never meet him. Almost daily she was in town, drinking coffee and smoking cigarettes in the hotel, circling the waterside pubs like a spinning top. A few times she came home drunk, once with a swollen jaw from a bike fall.

Nearly six weeks passed before she cornered Jason outside the post office. He said work was hectic, but he hadn't forgotten her. In fact he was delighted to see her and suggested they go to the hotel for a drink. After a few, they drove to the little beach on the peninsula and made love.

"I need to see you more often," Bobogue whispered. "At least once a week. You can come to my house. My brother won't mind."

"Look," said Jason, pulling away, "I'm really busy. When things quiet down I'll have more time."

"Can't you make time?"

"I'm not God."

The drive back to town was fast and bumpy. She wanted to know more about him: What was his work number? His mobile phone number? Where exactly did he live? Did he like her? Why wasn't he answering her questions?

"I'm tired," he said impatiently. "There's a lot going on at work, I told you that."

He dropped her outside the town and sped away. The evening was warm and the tide was full and calm. A couple of white yachts returned to harbour, and a rust-sailed hooker docked at the quay with a group of sunset watchers. People strolled on the pier and Bobogue heard a ceili band play through open windows of the hotel. Outside waterfront bars and cafes, couples in shorts and t-shirts sat at tables. She wished Jason and herself might do things like that: dine at sunset on seafood and champagne.

When she got to the Vespa, Bobogue couldn't find the ignition key and retraced her steps, peeling the ground as she backtracked. No luck, so she figured the key was either in Jason's car or at the beach. She walked home and stayed up late, searching in drawers and tins and bowls for a spare key she had put somewhere safe. No sign of it. She lit candles and offered a prayer to Saint Anthony as a last resort. Bobogue slept without inspiration and in the morning got a screwdriver and headed into town.

She was admiring the view at the top of Hogan's Hill when she heard a car approach from behind, and her face brightened when she recognised the white Volvo. She flagged joyfully, but Jason changed gears and passed her by. There was a woman in the passenger seat.

"Hey!" Bobogue shouted after the Volvo. "Hey!"

In the car, Jason's wife said, "Christ, that woman gives me the creeps. She came to my writing circle a few times. She's absolutely bonkers. We had to ask her to leave. I told you about her, she used staple her poetry to the lamp posts in town. The police had to stop her."

Jason swept down the valley, and Bobogue paled as the car telescoped away. He had ignored her. And he was with that stuck-up blow-in from the writing group. It struck her they might be husband and wife. She got weak and sat on the ditch.

Bobogue knew Jason's surname, but couldn't find his telephone number in the directory, and enquiries had no listing for him. She went demented and Paddy wondered if she was in need of help. She broke two chairs on the kitchen table one night, and spent hours screaming and swearing at the fire. Then she wept for a few days and slowly slipped into blue silence.

The tourists had thinned out before Bobogue spotted Jason in Maguire's supermarket one evening. She crossed the store to confront him but he vanished. Another time she saw him get petrol at The Rock filling station but he sped away as she approached. Matt the mechanic told her he lived down around Seafield.

Bobogue swore that no matter how long it took, or how many roads she traveled, she'd find him. Weekend after weekend, when workers rested at home, she trawled through Seafield, Barrtraw, Skyline and Trawroo for Jason's car. She peered into driveways, scowled at the designer houses with SUVs, Mercs, BMWs and Saabs. No white Volvo in the Blow-in Belt. But Bobogue soldiered on.

As the weather got wintry, she wore leather gloves and a parka for the cold. In mid-December the roads were icy by sundown and one Saturday she skidded twice coming down Skyline. She stopped at Maguire's Supermarket and got a six-pack for Paddy and a soldier of whiskey for herself. Christmas songs played over loudspeakers and the checkers wore Santa caps. Every few minutes the voice of Paddy Maguire interrupted the music with bargain announcements for turkey and ham, whiskey, cigarettes and mince pies. Bobogue was bagging her purchases when a shiny black car pulled outside. She saw Jason get out and hurry into the store; he didn't notice her in the hooded parka.

Jason left the bottle of wine and carton of ice cream on the passenger's seat and pulled out from Maguire's. He liked his new car.

He toyed with switches and controls, played a U2 CD, balanced the speakers. Over the weekend he'd hook his iPod to the system and he'd have music all the way to heaven.

When he spotted Bobogue's Vespa peeping out of Duffy's Lane, he drove faster. But turning down towards Kilmore, Jason thought he heard a rustle in the seat behind. Twisting his head, he caught a blurred movement with the corner of his eye, just before Bobogue grabbed him by the neck. He made a gurgling cry as the car swerved out of control. It mounted the ditch, screamed through hazel and birch, until stopped by a stonewall.

Jammed against the seat by a huge air bag, Jason moaned and wept. Bobogue climbed from the wreck and into a haze of smoke and road dust. Metal winced and creaked; one headlight beamed cock-eyed across the frost-white fields.

Uneasy on her feet, Bobogue walked towards town with blood on her face and hid in the ditch when cars approached. She had reached The Rock filling station when an ambulance sped by in a whirl of blue noise.

The streets were empty and the Church was full for Saturday night Mass. In the quiet, crisp darkness, Bobogue retrieved the booze she'd stashed in Maguire's wheelie bin and headed to Duffy's Lane. She smoked two cigarettes and had a few slugs of whiskey while staring at the stars. She mounted her red Vespa and it started on the second turn. Sore and slow on the icy roads, Bobogue rode home at ten miles an hour, a poem rising in her heart.

After Hours

IT WAS WELL PAST CLOSING TIME AND THE PUB WAS CROWDED, DARK and steamy. Monty Hogan staggered towards the counter, lost his balance, and fell on a table of drinkers. Men and women scrambled out of his way, toppling bottles and smashing glasses. Drinks splashed and a woman screamed that her dress was ruined. Another woman cried, "Fuck you Monty!"

Helpless as a babe in a cot, Monty lay across the table, clutching his frada—an electronic gadget that looked like a laptop computer affixed to a guitar neck. It blared head-wrecking psychedelic whirls.

"Stop that noise!" a man roared.

"Turn off the frada!" a women shouted. "Turn off the fuckin' frada!"

The frada screeched louder when two men lifted Monty off the table. Peter Egan, the publican, grabbed a syphon of soda water from a shelf and sprayed the flashing instrument. There was a sizzle, and Monty jolted, then collapsed on the floor, still clutching the silenced gadget.

"Don't touch him or ye'll get electrocuted!" warned Mossy Fossett. "Call d'ambulance!

"I'll call fuck all at this hour of the morn!" shouted Egan, "Drink up or shut up!"

Two Good Samaritans settled Monty on a bench. He was drenched in soda water. Lily Doyle felt his brow and took his pulse. "He's alive anyway," she announced, and a jumble of relief and disappointment rumbled around the pub.

1:25AM

Monty is forgotten and Lulu Hopal, the merriest widow in town, croons *Yesterday*. Her voice is ethereal at first, but gets distraught by the second verse. She veers off song and addresses her dead husband Faxo, asking why he had to go and spoil the show.

In tears, Mary White orders a gin and tonic, and Egan the landlord has to lower his head, to catch her whisper. Then she puts her tongue in his ear and kisses his cheek. Perks of the job, he fondles her breasts and she sighs, "You never visited me like you promised."

"Any night now," he muttered and turned away to fill a pint of porter for Oliver Collins, and another for himself.

Bart Carson, an undercover gossip, asked Egan if he'd heard the rumour about Bella Donnell and Father Wogan. He hadn't. He took a sharp draw on a fag when Bart said the priest tried to exorcise a demon from the ex-nun and failed. "She ended up on top of him," Bart whispered, clutching Egan's elbow. "The two of 'em were bollox naked when Mary Callinan came into the room with a Mass card for him to sign!"

Shaking his head, Egan turns away and fills two half-whiskeys for Dido Lavorn, a blonde hell-raiser, decades beyond her prime.

"Peter," she whispers, "if you want a bit of housework done any-time, just let me know."

"Sound," he nods, and lies that he has no ice.

1:42AM

Henry Connoly, a long time patron, sings *When the Swallows come back to Capistrano* and Sharon Jones holds Egan's hand over the counter and hums along in harmony. After the applause, from a dark corner near the Ladies, the sultry voice of Dodo Malley pleads, "Put your sweet lips a little closer to the phone..." Glasses clink in antic-ipation of a classic performance as she emerges from the darkness, singing from her heart, holding a small mixer bottle as a microphone: "I'll tell the mah-ha-haaan, to turn the jukebox way down lo-ho-hooo..."

Some other women wailed along and Egan wondered if he should call it a night and throw them all out before things turned chaotic. That happened once in a blue moon; things slipped out of order in a blink. Someone would fuck up, some one else would react and next there'd be an explosion. He pulled on a cigarette, slugged his pint and gauged the crowd. They were mostly well-on, but good-humoured. He'd let them be. Anyway, soon the dog race from Mexico would be on the television and he'd make a good till.

Egan squinted over at Monty, drew hard on the fag, and queried Henry Connoly,

"What kind of a yoke is that frada anyway?"

"Something he invented from bits a' computers an' electric guitars an' things. Monty's a genius."

"I know," Egan sighed, topping his pint and beginning one for Henry, "but the fucker is nuts. The rig-out of him...in a fuckin ballet dress an' a fur coat...isn't he getting dosh from NAMA?"

"Apparently every month he gets a thousand fedros or maybe more from them and all the pills and stuff that he can swallow."

"It's an amazing NAMA," Egan said cynically, "the rest of us payin' tax to keep the show on the road an' Monty inventing contraptions to drive us up the fuckin wall..."

"National Asset and Protected Personalities, I think that's the name of the fund he's drawin' from."

"Jesus wept."

"Well, I knew that scheme to monitise the arts was always going to be a disaster. Money down the drain. It's worse than the original NAMA. I mean, Monty and his likes add damn-all to the economy. They make this art shit and they're costing us a fortune. Give me a break."

"At least the builders built something and used up sand and timber and stuff. And they spent their money."

"Exactly, Peter. We're back to the Saints and Scholars, that's what we're famous for now. Geniuses like Monty, no more tar and cement. It's all art nowadays. Apparently that's what the tourists want to experience, the arts."

Egan lit a cigarette and said, "I don't know what tourist would want to come and visit Monty."

"Well, of course he's very talented," said Henry, "and he's a fine fella when he's not on a jag, very well-mannered and sociable, sensible dress ex-cetera, ex-cetera. Has afternoon tea in the Imperial Hotel with his mother and so on. And then he snaps...something gets to the poor hure and he goes astray bit by bit until he's gone totally gaga. Then Galligan gives him the needle and after a few days he's right as rain."

"He's gaga enough now," said Egan. "I mean...you could put up with the frada occasionally, if he could play it or turn the fuckin' volume down...anyone can get shit-faced once in a while, but havin' both of them full-on and he prancing around in the ballet get-up, now that shit can get to you."

"And of course you can't bar him or you'd have wan of them shaggin' anti-discrimination cops on your arse. But sure there's no harm in the poor hure, he's his own worst enemy. And who's to say that if we had a mother and father like Monty has, that we'd be any better than him. Worse maybe."

"NAMA has a lot to answer for."

2.05AM

Peggy Morgan came to the counter and ordered a small brandy and a bottle of Tarzan Extra. She was with her mother's lodger, Ms. McCabe, who worked for the dentist. Egan wondered if they were lovers or just friends. After serving her, he turned to Henry.

"Has she a NAMA deal as well?"

22

"She has indeed. Apparently she's a poet and gets a good slice of pie. Imagine! Did you know that, according to Fás, there are sixty-five registered poets in Ennis? Hah? More poets there now than Polish plasterers in the old days. Go figure that one out."

"Brutal. And I bet you, there's none of them as good a poet as Quaker Leary from Ballyfin," Egan said.

"My point exactly. The Quaker wouldn't go within an asses' roar of NAMA; he wouldn't take a penny from them. He paddles his own canoe. And for the record, there's twenty-two potters in Kilfadeen, all on the NAMA tit. I mean, how many jugs do you want on the dresser? Hah?"

"Twenty-two blue cuckoos," said Egan, filling a pint for himself, "And you heard that Mattie Clark got on the Leprechaun Scheme? I mean, more luck to the poor devil, but do we need another fuckin' leprechaun in this parish? Like, we have at least a dozen of 'em."

"My point exactly. But you see, Peter, we're a tourist nation now, we're in arts and entertainment. Tourists expect to meet leprechauns and talk to them, watch them do tricks with a crock of brass coins. But most of these shagging leprechauns spend their days on the beer. And a more awkward bunch of flutes you won't meet in a month of Sundays. In my opinion they're a liability to the place, they're giving us a bad name. I mean, how can it serve us well, to be known as the leprechaun capital of the world? Give me a break! Cut them off! The same goes for that terrible bore, MacClune the shanachie, he's another NAMA beneficiary, another national asset, an' a most toxic one. I cringe every time I see him giving a spiel to tourists, and he hanging around Doyle's Corner with a caubeen and a clay pipe. Straight from Disneyland. You see, they get paid for this shit. They're all artists now, Peter."

2:20AM

"What gets me most about this art stuff," confided Egan, "is that it's impossible to know the good from the bad. Like, you know if a carpenter hangs a door the wrong way, but this art stuff is different."

"Aha!" said Henry. "You put your finger on the crux of the matter. With art, there is no good or bad. Not anymore. I always said there should be a regulator for the arts."

"But you know, I blame Labour and the Greens. When they were in government, the whole shebang went belly-up."

"I agree. NAMA should have stuck to the property problem; letting them near the arts was ludicrous. But that was the Greens, that was the Greens. And once NAMA sold the Book of Kells to Google, we were shagged. After that, everything was on the table. I know it got us out of a hole at the time, but..."

"Well of course, that was let go because of the whole church scandal but then they sold the Cliffs of Moher to Microsoft, who hung a big fuckin' sign on it that you can see from New York! What's all that about?" Egan asked.

"My point exactly!" Henry said, beckoning for another pint. "We became a brand: Good old Ireland of the *grá mo chroí* welcomes. *Céad Míle Fáilte* and all that shit. You see, even though Labour and the Greens were top-heavy with brains, they were no match for Google or Microsoft or Don Draper."

Egan nodded. He knew Henry was getting loaded, but he was good enough for a few more pints, so he put another one in front of him. "None of them were as smart as poor ol' Charlie Haughey, bad and all as he was," he said.

"My point exactly!" Henry said.

A woman named Kiki O'Neill was singing 'Two Little Orphans' and the pub roared the chorus. Brutal stuff. Henry said she had a NAMA deal—she sang five hundred songs a year and got big money for it. A microchip sent a message back to Apple every time she sang, he said, and money went straight into her bank account in Kilrush.

"It's all microchips and PIN numbers now," complained Egan.

"My point exactly!" said Henry. "We're owned by Google, Amazon, Microsoft and Apple, like it or lump it. They know where we live, what we ate. We're fuckin' guinea pigs, Peter, and they're watching us. Monty explained it all to me one night. Bad and all as poor old Monty is, at least he's a genius, and I really don't begrudge him the Elite Plan he has. In all fairness, the likes of him need to be supported."

2:35AM
The Geek Hynes, a thirty-year-old unemployed nerd, had been eavesdropping and said,

"What's wrong with a poet or a singer getting a NAMA deal? NAMA helped all the big crooks, didn't they?"

"But tis gone too far," Egan said and Henry nodded. "I mean, there's a fella in Barrana who got a NAMA deal to make statues out of old telegraph poles with a chainsaw."

"My point exactly!" said Henry. "And they gave thousands to

that nut Babbler Forrester to compose a concerto! I mean that guy hasn't a note in his head! What was that Shakespeare said about the monkey and the typewriter? Oh damn, it escapes me now…but it's the same thing."

"The reality is, this country is just an anthill now," the Geek said. "We're all drones, bringing home bacon for the queens. The Eurocrats own us. We should have revolted when the Celtic Tiger imploded. We needed a program like the WPA that the Yanks had during the Depression. But we had to reinvent the wheel and fucked it up. Anyway, we can't blame the Brits for the disaster—we showed the world we were well able to crucify ourselves. We believed our own blarney! The joke is on us."

Egan moved down the counter to serve Dilly Mangan. He only tolerated the Geek because he needed him to hack the till now and again to get around the NAMA taxes. The landlord figured the Geek was too bright for his own good, and too thirsty as well. A tipsy woman was singing "Wooden Heart" in the dark. Dixie Daly, an amateur jockey, harmonized in the chorus. Egan wondered if they too had NAMA deals. The Guinness clock over the bar read 2.45 am. Soon the greyhound race would be broadcast from Cancun, so he filled himself a pint, lit a cigarette and took a black ledger from under the counter.

2.50AM

Henry calls for two pints, and the anticipation of free porter puts The Geek on a roll. Egan begins filling the order and listens to him telling Henry, "We'd be in a different Ireland now, if the proletariat had taken to the streets when the shit first hit the fan. We took it lying down. Are we destined to be always picking up the tab for an elite?"

"My point exactly," muttered Henry, looking at the floor. Egan topped the two pints and left them on the counter. Henry put a fistful of money beside them and said, "That's the bank."

"*Sláinte*, Henry." saluted the Geek. He took a drink, smacked his lips and said, "We have a weak gene, which we indulge, rather than taking responsibility for it. We're suckers for fairytales. Deep down we believe the crock of gold and the rainbow crap. We're weaned and reared on it. So at any given time, a certain percentage of the population are away with the fairies, whether they be the politicians or their followers or both. How else could the same clots be voted into government, election after election? We fall for the bait every time. We have a societal rot."

Egan exhaled loudly and lit a cigarette. He knew The Geek would like a smoke, but didn't offer him one.

"What do you mean by societal rot?" Henry asked politely.

"A suspension of critical faculties," said the Geek. "We are no longer independent thinkers, we do our master's bidding. We might as well be on a Roman slave galley. We're all paddling, so guys can have chauffeurs and yachts and stuff."

"All I know," Egan sighed, "is that I'm being screwed." And nodding to The Geek, he said, "I'll need you to give me a hand with the books for the race."

"Absolutely. No problem, Peter," the nerd said, straightening his tie.

3.00AM

A harmonica played a few lonesome notes that segued into *Dirty Old Town*. Right on cue, Lulu Hoppal warbled, "I met my lo-ho-ho-hove by the gasworks wall....Dreamed a dreee-ee-eeaaam…" The bar howled and Egan picked up the remote control gizmo and zapped on the television. Without warning, Lance Piggott of CNN loudly announced to the pub that killer bees were on the rampage in Zagrastan. The singing faltered, and everyone looked at the buzzing plague on the maxi screen above the fireplace. Enough of that. Egan clicked the remote and surfed his drinkers to Al-Jazeera, BBC, a Korean cooking show, a jewelry auction in Boston. A roar erupted from the pub when he clicked to Telemundo Mexacali 12, broadcasting the Mexican Open Greyhound Grand Prix live from Ortega Stadium in Cancun.

3:06AM

Flickering television light and spatters of Spanish enter Monty's brain and he regains consciousness slowly. To determine his where-abouts, he opens an eyelid with caution. He sees everyone in the pub staring at the screen, where tall women paraded dogs. The pub's eyes search for Ballygale Bandit, the local greyhound, owned by John Joe Mac, trained by Murty Kerins and sponsored by NAMA.

"Which wan is he?" asked Dodo Malley.

"Number four, the brindle dog with the lady in the tricolour." pointed Egan.

"I hope she comes home with them," Henry said. "she'd warm me up on a winter's night."

"Jaysus, but that's very like Miko Kelly there in the front with the red shirt," Egan said, as shots of the spectators appear.

"Fuck me, it is!" cried Mary White, "and that's Maggie Kane and Dolores beside him."

Betting Odds Flashed on the screen:
La Bamba 3/1
El Greco Grande 5/2
Senor Castro 2/1
Ballygale Bandit 3/2
Coca Dolce 1/1
Chi Yung 3/2

Egan lowered the volume and announced,

"I'm openin' a book now if anyone's interested in having an interest in the race."

"I'll put five on the Chinese dog," Bart Hogan said, tossing five fedros on the counter.

"I'll do ten on the Bandit," Packie Lamb said.

"Fuck the begrudgers," Laya Lohan said, "I'll do the same."

"Me too," a woman in red agreed.

A crush formed at the bar as Egan took the punters' money. He wrote in his black book and called out numbers to The Geek, who scribbled dockets for the bets.

3:10AM

The hum of betting and clamour of drinking invades Monty's head and his body heats up. The frada warms accordingly and clicks into life, quiet as a late night fridge. His mind begins to speed as thoughts hurtle through like shooting stars. His fingers tap on the instrument's track pad. Dog, dog, he mutters, dog, dog. Suddenly the frada emits a bark that startles the pub.

"What the fuck was that?" Egan asked.

"Sounded like a dog," Henry muttered.

"Must be outside," Duddy Nixon said, placing two fedros on Señor Castro, because his brother lived in a place named like that in San Francisco.

"Dogs can pick up the fever," Oliver Collins said, "you know …the vibe like…dogs always want to get in on the action…they're like bankers and lawyers and the rest of them…"

3:25AM

Egan closes the book and makes a phone call to lay off his bets. The Geek has the remote control gizmo and turns up the volume. On the screen, the women lead the dogs to their traps, to a fanfare of trumpets. The pub is tense and silent, all eyes on the race.

A bell clangs, and an electric hare zooms down the track. Dogs yelp and traps shoot open as the ball of fur darts by. In the background the race commentator Diego Avilia rattles in Spanish. Monty stands to get a better view of the screen and meanders to the counter. He picks up Henry Connoly's pint and has a slug. Nobody sees him; the race has their full attention.

In front from the break, Señor Castro soon had a length on El Greco, who was followed closely by Chi Yung and Ballygale Bandit.

Behind them came La Bamba and Cosa Dolce. The pub cheered on Ballygale, but he pulled back after the first bend and fell to last place. He slowed to a canter, then a dance. A split screen showed dogs racing in one screen and the Bandit waltzing in the other. The commentator rattled faster.

"Fuckin' hell!" exclaimed Egan.

"He's doped," Geek said.

"This is...this is fuckin' crazy!" cried Egan.

Ballygale Bandit was dancing in front of millions of viewers on satellite tv. The pub erupted in shouting and swearing, and firing threats at the greyhound.

Monty was tapping the frada. There was something he should be doing...something concerning the dog on the television. Something to do with the microchip he implanted in the dog's ear last week. Something to do with the frada. Something to do with NAMA.

"Oh no!" he shrieked and suddenly pecked at keys on the frada.

The television screen turned black. Green strings of computer code flashed on it; barks and static farted from the speakers. The Geek fiddled with the remote, but it made no difference. Egan grabbed the controls and clicked impatiently. More of the same. Then someone noticed Monty frantically toggling switches and knobs on the frada. They screamed at him to stop.

Henry grabbed Monty as he hit a power chord with full reverb. Suddenly, the screen filled with the head of a greyhound: Ballygale Bandit, tongue pumping, and the pub forgot about Monty. They watched the Bandit clocking eighty miles an hour and leading Chi

31

Yung by a shoulder coming into the last bend. They cheered for the home-dog, and wild as Hendrix, Monty worked up steam, pushing the frada to the max. He was drowned out by the roar that went up as Ballygale Bandit pulled away on the home stretch and finished almost two lengths ahead of the field.

While everyone cheered and hugged and laughed in the pub, Monty powered down the frada and wiped his brow on the sleeve of the fur coat. He lifted a pint from the counter and had a good slug out of it.

"Jesus," he whispered to Henry, "I almost fucked that up, man. The Bandit was supposed to do the dance at the end—you know, at the prize presentation. I can't even remember the fuckin' code for the dance now. But fuck it, who gives a shit, right? We won, right?"

Henry nodded and prised the pint from his hand.

"That dog was carrying a lot of cash," Monty whispered. "NAMA would have hung my ass if I fucked up. But I didn't, see? I didn't fuck-up, and we won, right? Monty might be fucked-up but he doesn't fuck-up. Right? I'm not like the developers, right?"

He tapped the frada and two horrendous barks froze the jubilant pub. In the silent vacuum Monty politely asked,

"May I please have a pint, Mr. Egan, to toast our local greyhound's victory."

Exhaling a cone of smoke, Egan shook his head and said,

"Sorry Monty, you've had enough. Yourself and your frada nearly fucked up everything here tonight, not just once or twice, but several times."

"But we won, didn't we?" pleaded Monty. "Only for the frada, this fucking country would be bankrupt again tomorrow. And that fucking dog would be in a taco. What have you against my frada? Where's your vision, man? Where's your vision?"

BLUE MONEY

SUNDAY AFTERNOON WAS WARM AND LAZY AND THOSE WHO could, went to the seaside. Deep in the glen below the town, John and Marty fished by an old chestnut tree that arched over the bank, darkening the water with its shadow. Only quiet river sounds dimpled the stillness: the distant pop of a rising trout, the worried hoot of a water hen in the reeds.

Rods resting on the grass verge, they sat against the tree and watched their floats. Bored and penniless, they were sixteen and just finished school for the summer. Marty flicked a pebble into the water and said, "What d'you think of knockin' off those donation boxes in the church?"

"For fuck's sake," John muttered, "you can't be serious?"

"It's handy dosh and..."

Marty stopped when he heard voices approach. John heard them too, the giggles of young women. Linking each other, a pair of young ladies strolled up the tree-lined riverbank.

"Jesus," whispered John, "who're these two?"

They were strangers. One wore a wide-brimmed straw hat, tight white t-shirt and shorts; the other had a purple bandanna around her head, black halter-top and denim mini-skirt.

"Christ," muttered Marty, "look at the legs of 'em."

Engrossed in their own conversation, the women didn't notice the youths peering from behind the tree until they were ten steps away. They quietly exchanged 'hellos' and the one in the straw hat called,

"Catch any fish?"

"No," the lads replied in unison.

"What are you fishing for anyway?"

"Trout, fluke, eels…whatever," Marty said.

"Would any of you have a cigarette?"

"No," said Marty and John shook his head.

The women joined them and hunkered down on the bank by the tree. Out-of-state by their accents, older than the youths by a few years.

"I'm Suzy," the straw hatted one said, "and this is my friend Blue."

The boys introduced themselves and smiled shyly.

"Are ye on holidays?" Marty asked.

"You could say that," Blue replied, "are you locals?"

"Yeah, we're from the town," Marty nodded.

"Beautiful little place," Suzy said, "you live in a lovely part of the country."

"Are ye staying in bed and breakfast?" Marty inquired.

"No," Blue said, "we're camping."

"Good weather for it," mumbled John, his eyes on the fishing line, too shy to look at the strangers. Marty took side glances at them

35

and noticed neither wore a bra. Their legs were bronzed and shapely and his heart bombed when he looked right up between Blue's thighs and saw no underwear. She caught him peeping and when their eyes met, she grinned and he quickly turned away and fumbled with his fishing rod.

"If you catch any fish," she said, "can we have some?"

"Sure," Marty said and John nodded.

"We're camping in the little wood below," Suzy said, pointing downstream, "so if you get lucky, you know where we are..."

"Okay," Marty smiled and the women left, talking quietly as they strolled down the riverside path.

"Jesus Christ, what do you make of that?" Marty whispered.

John shook his head quickly and blurted,

"Fine things, aren't they?"

"For fuck's sake, they're mad for the ride...no bras or knickers or anything...fish my arse...it's fellas they want..."

They caught no fish, though they waited under the chestnut tree for another couple of hours. Women on their minds, they returned home for Sunday tea when the Angelus pealed from the church across the river.

Later that evening they hung outside the chip-shop, looking down towards the river, wondering what the women were doing, where they were from, why did they come here, above all places. As the sun went down, Marty became frustrated. "Listen, they want us to ride them...I bet they're waiting below in the wood for us."

"We can't just walk in on them."

The Sunday drinkers came to town and packed the few pubs, livening the summer's night with the rumpus of card playing and dart throwing. Marty rambled on about the things he was going to do when he became a man: drink, gamble and bed as many women as he could. "It's the only job," he muttered, kicking his toes against a telegraph pole, "that's what we're here for."

When they went to the river the next morning, Marty had a pack of cigarettes he nicked from his mother's handbag. The weather was heavy and overcast and looked like it could rain at any time.

"It might be a good day for fish," John said, as they cast their lines by the chestnut tree.

"Let's leave the rods here and go down the wood to these dames," Marty urged.

They strode in single file, Marty leading. Wild woodbine and rambling rose scented the air with anticipation. Marty stopped at the old stone bridge and said quietly,

"I want the one with the straw hat, you can have the other one."

"Blue?" John whispered and Marty nodded.

Eyes scanning for sign of the camp, ears perked for female sound, they followed a path by a rattling brook and went deeper into the wood. Finches fretted, blackbirds fled and a grey heron rasped from an oak tree as they passed below. They smelled smoke, heard voices in the distance. Marty grinned, gave the thumbs-up sign and moved quicker.

Suzy was bathing naked in the stream when they came into the campsite.

"The fishermen!" she greeted and Blue stood up from a small crackling fire, a blackened can in her hand.

"Any fish?" she asked.

Marty shook his head. "Not yet," he smiled, "but we brought ye cigarettes." He looked at Suzy, sitting in the water. He'd never before seen a nude woman in the flesh and his whole body tingled.

John glanced at the fire and the makeshift camp: a sheet of brown tarpaulin draped over a fallen tree. The others spoke but he hardly heard them, his eyes roaming over the objects hanging from sticks impaled in the soft ground: a dead crow, rabbit skins, a long yellowed bone, a cow's skull with one horn. He wanted to retreat but Blue was offering him tea. "Hope you don't mind drinking from a jam jar."

"I'm fine," he muttered.

Suzy came dripping from the stream and Marty drooled as she dried herself with a torn towel. He opened the pack of cigarettes and offered them around. Everyone took one except John. Suzy teased him and he blushed. "We were going to come down last night," Marty said, blowing a smoke ring.

"You should have," Blue said, "we love company."

Marty smiled and sat on a stone by the fire. "So do we," he chuckled, "nothing happens in the town...it's dead as a graveyard." John nodded, testing sentences in his head.

"Are ye staying long?" he asked, eventually.

"It depends," Suzy replied, buttoning a long shirt that came to her thighs.

"Yeah, it depends," agreed Blue.

"Ye've a grand spot here," Marty said, offering another round of cigarettes.

"Can I take a few of these for later?" Blue asked.

"No problem," Marty said and gave her four.

"You're really nice guys," Suzy smiled.

A slight breezed rustled the treetops overhead and heavy drops of rain pattered on the leaves. John looked skywards and said,

"I better get back to the fishing rods."

"They're alright," assured Marty, "stay where you are; you'll get drenched."

But his mind was made up and he dashed away.

Back by the chestnut tree John watched the river boil in the heavy rain, peeping down the path every once in a while for Marty. He waited an hour, then another before his mate appeared running, a delirious grin on his face.

"They'll ride," he panted, "I asked them...they'll do it."

"Jesus!"

"Yeah...anytime, they said, but we'll have to pay them."

"Pay them?"

"Yeah...they're broke...they want fifty euros."

"Are you serious? Are they...are they prostitutes or something?"

"No...they're just broke."

Marty went to the church that evening and knelt at the back near the statue of Martin de Porres. He waited for the worshipers to disperse after Benediction and slipped into a confessional when Joe Tobin, the sacristan was at the altar quenching candles. In the dark he heard Joe swish by, greeting statues as he passed, saying a prayer here, making a request there. He heard the heavy doors creak shut and the lock snap home. Then the church was quiet and peaceful, apart from the rain drumming on the roof.

When Marty left the confessional, the air held ghost smells of quenched candles and incense. Empty and bigger than he had ever seen it, the church was dimly lit by evening light coming through the stained glass window behind the altar and the flickering red glow from the sanctuary lamp. He went to the wooden Vincent de Paul collection box and lifted it. Disappointed that it was so light, he wondered if there was more money in the Foreign Missions box under the statue of Saint Patrick. That was heavier alright, and with a box under each arm he went into the sacristy and out through a window.

In the graveyard behind the church he tried to force the boxes open with his penknife but the blade broke. "Fuck," he muttered, "fuck, fuck, fuck."

He looked at the church clock: it was nearly nine. The girls would be waiting; John would be waiting. He'd better hurry. But he couldn't walk over the bridge and through the town carrying two collection boxes. Better to cross the river below the cascades, on the stepping-stones the poachers used to snatch salmon.

The river was swollen and the stepping stones were almost covered by the flood. He took off his shoes, tied them together by the laces and slung the brogues around his neck. A box under each arm, he stepped on the stones, wary as a tightrope walker. Water rushed against his feet and halfway across, he felt it hard to keep his balance

40

and wondered about turning back. He glanced around and saw Tobin the sacristan on the bridge above, waving madly.

Downstream by the old chestnut tree, John sat between Suzy and Blue. He felt uncomfortable and wished Marty would arrive soon. It was almost twilight and the river was running fast and urgent with the flood. Rubbish and debris from the town floated past and then on its own, like a baby's coffin, the wooden Vincent de Paul box. John recognised it and said,

"He'll be here soon."

"Good."

"You sure you got no cigarettes?" Suzy pressed.

They waited another ten minutes or so and then the women suggested John to go and look for his friend.

"He owes me for a favour," Blue said, "I want my money."

"Otherwise we're taking these rods," Suzy said.

Hurrying upstream towards town, John stopped when he saw dusky shapes by a pool called the Salmon Hole. From their helmets and caps he picked out the silhouettes of policemen and firemen. He saw them haul something heavy from the river. A body. John's heart thumped. He watched from behind a tree and saw the men take off their headgear and bless themselves. He blessed himself too and wondered if a poacher had fallen in and drowned. Names flipped through his mind. That's what's delaying Marty, he thought, he'll arrive when all this drama is over.

Couples

THE SITTING ROOM WAS WARM AND SERENE, WITH A TRACE OF jasmine incense. The radio whispered classical music from Lyric FM, and Mona balanced her checkbook on a beanbag near the fire. In an armchair across the hearth, her husband Rolf frowned at a Picasso print on the wall: *War and Peace*. He looked preoccupied, a bundle of typed pages on his lap.

"I got a call from Dermot today," he said quietly, "Kate moved out."

"What?"

"Kate moved out. She left Dermot."

"Jesus Christ! Why didn't you tell me before now?"

"I was waiting for the right time."

"But Jesus Christ Rolf, she's my best friend!"

"I know."

"When did this happen?"

"Yesterday."

"Oh my God. This is incredible. I spoke with her on Sunday and she didn't say anything. What happened?"

"Apparently she met someone else. Dermot never knew. She told him as she was packing."

"And she left just like that?"

He nodded and went to the kitchen for a bottle of wine.

Mona looked at the small black and white photo on the mantelpiece from a college ball: Rolf and herself with Dermot and Kate. The couples had been best friends since way back then. Kate was shy, Dermot was loose, Rolf was stiff and Mona was somewhere in between. "I can't believe this," she whispered.

They had known each other forever, stuck around town after graduating and became part of the arts scene. Dermot worked as producer in a local radio station; Rolf was editor of a community paper and Mona had a small craft shop in a renovated mill by the waterfront. Kate taught creative writing at the university.

"I'm shocked," she muttered when Rolf returned with the bottle, "Jesus Christ, we never know what's going on in someone's life."

He nodded and poured two glasses of wine.

"But I can't imagine her with anyone apart from Dermot," Mona said.

"It seems she was seeing this guy for the last three months. He's Spanish, a chef in the college canteen."

"Holy shit."

"They're moving to Alicante."

"Jesus! Alicante! What's the matter with her?"

A few nights later, Dermot came over for dinner. He spilled his heart out and Mona went to bed early, leaving the two men to drink and talk until dawn. He came again the following week, and told them he had received a letter from Kate's lawyer – she wasn't coming back and wanted to sell their house. He cried at dinner and got drunk and conked out on the sitting room sofa. They worried about him, and Mona wrote to Kate through her solicitor, hoping to coax her to her senses. When she received no response after three weeks, she wrote again.

"I don't believe this," she said to Rolf, "I mean, I thought we were best friends."

Through six months of legal ping-pong, Dermot came for dinner at least once a week. They listened and consoled him, gave him heart and support. They read the small print in legal documents and helped him fight his corner. They cajoled him into to going to concerts with them, brought him to the Arts Festival reception and tried to humour him out of his sorrows. It was their idea that he should buy a small apartment down by the harbour when it was all over. Make a fresh start, they said, everything will be fine, you're a young man in your prime.

After the divorce was finalised and all bonds were untied, he took their advice and bought an apartment. A one bedroom box, with a balcony overlooking the docks, it faced south and had a view of the Blue Mountains over the roofs of warehouses. He moved in on his thirty-seventh birthday, and Mona and Rolf came by with two bottles of champagne to warm the home and celebrate his new age. He didn't sleep for hours after they left and got up several times to look at the boats in the harbour. In the morning, he sat on the floor and had a breakfast of coffee and cornflakes. He opened the windows and smelled the sea, played CDs of songs from his youth.

As Dermot settled into his new home, he came over to Rolf and Mona's less frequently, though the two men had lunch together at least once a week. His social life got hectic as summer came to town, and Rolf heard he was living life full throttle, meeting women from Italy, Spain, Poland and Ukraine. There were Americans too, a divorcee from Mayo and an exotic ballet dancer from Birr.

"I trust you're using rubbers," Rolf remarked, hearing of a threesome.

"Several," his friend smiled.

Dermot came over for a barbecue on the August holiday weekend. A god-sent balmy evening, they lingered outside and finished four bottles of Aldi wine before the night chilled. Back inside, Mona lit a token fire in the sitting room and made Irish coffees. Late into the night, Dermot gave a dramatic recitation of the 'Ballad of Reading Gaol'. Rolf corrected what he said was a misquoted line and that somehow led to an argument between them. Voices were raised. Mona ordered Dermot to cool down.

He looked at her with hurt eyes, walked out and banged the door.

Then he stuck his head back in and shouted,

"You've become fucking yuppies!"

The couple talked about the incident in the morning and Mona said Dermot owed them an apology. Rolf said, "Look, the guy was drunk. He was just letting off steam...he's been through a lot. Let's pretend it never happened."

Dermot and Rolf didn't have lunch the following week, or the week after that. August rolled on without contact and Mona said, "You should write to that jerk and demand an apology."

"Actually I was wrong, I looked up the poem. He was correct. If anything, it's us who owe him an apology. I intend writing to him."

"But he called us fucking yuppies, Rolf."

"Look. Forget it. It'll sort itself out. Ok?"

In late September they went on holidays to Greece. Rolf hated the resort, a noisy seaside town in Lesbos, packed with British and German tourists. They had a studio apartment in a large complex at the edge of town, and he was unnerved by young Greeks on motorcycles whenever they walked to the beach. The sand was littered with cigarette butts and drinking straws. The sun was merciless and Rolf brooded in the shade of a rented umbrella.

The Dermot issue followed them to Greece, and when Mona raised it one night at dinner, Rolf snapped. "For Christ's sake Mona, can't you forget the bloody thing while we're on holidays?"

"I just want to resolve it."

He was boiling and she thought he was going to explode like an over-inflated balloon. She pulled back from the table in alarm. He called a waiter and ordered a brandy and a cigar. For the rest of the evening they ignored each other, and when she got up next morning he was gone. An unsigned note left on the table read: *I'm taking off for a few days on my own.*

At first she was furious, and spent the day sipping brandy frappes outside the Lazy Fish taverna on the waterfront. That bastard won't spoil my holiday, she resolved. Greek youths passed like golden godettes. A flush of freedom lulled over her: singledom in the sun. Siesta sex. No, no, she couldn't do it. But it would be good enough for him, and the thought warmed her. After that she tanned in the sun by the pool in the apartment complex and dreamed of sin, over ouzo and coke.

Two days before they were due to leave for home, Rolf returned. It was late afternoon and the plaza by the pool was crowded and smelled of chlorine and body lotion. He picked his way around sunbeds until he spotted Mona sitting under a canvas parasol. She was chatting to a tanned Euroman with bleached hair. Rolf stopped, he saw them clink cocktail glasses. His mouth dried up and he turned away quickly.

Later that night they were both drunk when they met in the apartment. He called her a whore and she slapped him across the face and said he was a wimp. They stared at each other, breathing heavily like animals. No more words were spoken. Rolf backed away and spent the night on balcony, sleeping on a sun chair.

Their journey home was silent. Autumn had set in and Mona lit the sitting room fire and turned on the central heating at night. For a week they barely spoke and then one evening at dinner she said,

"Look, I'm sorry I went on about that incident with Dermot. Maybe we should try and patch things up with him...maybe I should call and invite him over."

"Why? Do you want to fuck him?"

He stared so hard at her that she dropped her cutlery and fled from the table.

They slept apart after that, and the house didn't lighten until Rolf went away for a few days. When he came back, he stopped using the sitting room and went straight to bed in the evening. Every Friday night he came home drunk and Mona found him asleep at the kitchen table on a couple of Saturday mornings. By Christmas she was seeing a therapist.

Dermot partied most weekends and the carpet in his apartment was stained, and the door to the shower was buckled. A French woman he took home refused to leave for two days. The following week his Mayo lover dropped by when he was entertaining someone else, and the two Donnas fought on the floor like cats until security men arrived. He drank and cavorted at full belt, seeing no end to the party. He was a free man and he was going to taste every fruit in Paradise. But fate had other plans. Dressed as a one-eyed pirate for the Arts Ball, he stumbled down the steps of the Silver Bay Hotel and cracked his ankle. He was out of work for a month and came back with a cane. That brought a cooling period and a time of forced reflection.

He was resting up one night, mindlessly watching the news on television, when Rolf arrived unannounced. His face was flushed and he extended his hand in friendship. Dermot shook it and invited him inside.

"Well it's good to see you, Rolf," he said, taking two cans of cider from the fridge.

"Sorry it took so long…"

"I often meant to call, but you know the way life goes."

Rolf nodded with a smile. He eased back on the couch and said, "Well I come with good news. I'm in love."

"What? What did you say?"

"I'm in love," Rolf beamed.

It happened in Greece while he was away from Mona. He was drinking alone in a beach club, watching a few women dance. One of them in particular held his eyes—a tall dark-haired lady in tight white jeans and orange t-shirt. She magnetized him and he got up and danced beside her.

"Christ Rolf, I can't imagine you discoing."

"Well I did…beside this beautiful woman…I invited her to have a drink and we got chatting."

Catriona was from Paris, and married to a mathematician, she told him almost immediately. She was a photographer, on the island on assignment for a travel magazine. When the club closed, they strolled along the shore. A blue moon hung over Turkey, a gentle sea lapping at their feet. They talked for hours and walked back to her hotel at dawn. But she declined to take Rolf inside or even kiss him goodbye.

They met again next evening and went for a meal at a

taverna in a small mountain village she knew. There was singing and dancing by old men with proud white mustaches and women with red scarves. Surrounded by feta cheese and olives, Rolf felt the spirit of old Greece through wine and ouzo. He melted into the most wonderful night of his life.

"I fell in love. And we didn't even kiss."

"Jesus. Does Mona know?"

Rolf shook his head, drank from his can.

"Not yet," he said, "anyway, it gets better. I arrived home smitten by Catriona. I had her business card and wrote to her, but she didn't reply. I phoned a few times but only got her voice mail. I left messages of course, but she never returned my calls."

After a month Rolf flew to Paris and went to her address. From a bench down the street he watched the apartment. Occasionally he glimpsed blurred bodies behind lace curtains. When it got dark he saw her silhouette on the shades, saw her husband's silhouette. Saw the light go out.

"I can't express how emotional I felt," he told Dermot, "On top of everything, I was ashamed of myself for snooping on her."

Next morning, some distance from the apartment, he approached Catriona as she walked to work. She was bewildered to see him and agreed to have coffee, even though she was running late. He bared his soul and she lit a cigarette and sighed, "Look, you're a lovely man, but I'm in love with a lovely man already. Please leave me alone."

Rolf went back to Ireland brokenhearted and a few weeks later he returned to Paris. He approached her on the way home from work but she refused to talk with him and threatened to call the police. Rolf pleaded with her but she ran away, shouting in French. Back at home he wrote and apologized, promised never to bother her again. After that he was overwhelmed by sadness and loneliness.

"And why didn't you say something?" Dermot asked.

"I couldn't. There was nothing to say. Until two weeks ago, that is—I got a letter from her, a note really. She just wrote *Are you there?*"

Rolf's eyes glinted like crystals in the sun.

"I'm in love," he said, "and I wasn't even looking for love. I've just been to Paris and Catriona and myself had a magical time together. I'm divorcing Mona."

"Jesus! I'd take it a bit slower if I were you."

Rolf nodded patiently and said,

"I have never been more certain about anything in my life. We're meant for each other and we're in love."

"Well, congratulations...I'm flabbergasted."

"There will be some to-ing and fro-ing between here and Paris for a while. Then Catriona will probably move here."

Winter winds and hail attacked the harbour town and Dermot's apartment was like a ship's bridge in a storm. Fishing boats were tied four deep at the quay and the clinking of cables against masts, kept him awake half of the night. Constant gale warnings, the days never seemed to brighten beyond stone grey. He called Rolf at work a few times but he was away. Then he received a postcard from Paris; Rolf was helping Catriona pack her stuff and move to Ireland.

On a wet March evening, as Dermot walked home from the radio station, he met Mona outside McFadden's Supermarket. Hidden in a dark wool coat, a fur Cossack hat down to her eyebrows, she was ashen-faced.

"Did you hear?" she asked, with eyes full of hurt, "He left me."

Dermot hugged her and patted her back. She shuddered into sobs and he linked her to a doorway, out of the path of shoppers and homegoing workers. He held her while she cried on his shoulder. He whispered that he understood, he understood. She sniffled herself together and said quietly,

"Thanks Dermot, I'm fine now."

They went into Neylon's Bar and sat in a small private snug that had a blazing turf fire. Dermot ordered hot whiskeys and Mona told her story. They had another drink.

"He just walked out," she muttered, "he told me to keep the fucking house...I hear they're renting a place in Ballyboy."

"Christ, I'm sorry Mona."

"Well you know what it's like, you've been through it too."

They fell silent. A clock ticked solemnly somewhere in the pub. The fire murmured up the chimney. From the bar came quiet mutters of conversation, clinking bottles, clunk and hiss of beer pumps. A smoker's cough. Coins being counted on the counter. The clock chimed eight. Dermot gently put his hand on Mona's.

"Would you like another drink?" he asked.

"Yeah," she said with a tear-eyed smile, "why not?"

WHEN EVERYONE IN BALLYJAMES HAD HELICOPTERS

THE ROAD FROM MULLA TO BALLYJAMES IS BARELY WIDE ENOUGH for two cars to pass each other, and miles of it weave along the northern face of the Killgory Mountains, through pine forest and high bog. The region is remote, sparsely populated by small farmers and a few reclusive artists who live in the hills.

About halfway between Mulla and Ballyjames, the pine forest falls away like stage curtains and Logra Lake appears unexpectedly. From the mountain behind, a waterfall pours into the lake, and the view is so spectacular, that the county council created a roadside vista area with two picnic tables and a litterbin. There is a small country store across the road from the vista area. Petty's of Logra has been there for generations, catering to basic needs of the locals. A sleepy, two-story building with white walls, green windows and shop front, it doubles as a post office. Apart from Wednesday, business is very slow and sometimes the shop is shut for hours. Occasionally it might not open at all for a day or two.

Wednesday is doleday, and in the morning, recipients come to collect their allowance at the post office and buy a few provisions in the shop. A police car is always there with two officers, who bring the money and the departmental documentation. With a dozen or so local recipients, mostly small farmers, everyone knows everybody else and it's as much a social gathering as an official roll call.

It's a busy day for Paddy Petty – busy in the post office and busy in the shop. Dole day provides his week's wages and he juggles hats as postmaster, shopkeeper and government paymaster. Medium height, eternally dressed in old blue suit, shirt and tie, Paddy uses Brylcreem to sculpt his dark wavy hair and tame his bushy eyebrows. Nearly fifty and fighting against it, he was once married, but his wife left a decade ago. She told him she was going to visit her sister in London and he drove her to the airport but never saw her again. She blew away like an autumn leaf, writing him a goodbye card from Southhampton. When people asked where she was, Paddy said she'd gone and joined the nuns and eventually they stopped asking. Nowadays he received comfort from Goldi, a hippie from the other side of the Killgory Mountains. Goldi swapped him free-range eggs and organic carrots for tobacco and chocolate. She was easy on his head and stayed with him once a month, often for three or four nights.

In late May, a few strangers turned up to collect dole at the post office. Scruffy young men and women, dressed in leather, they had odd hairstyles, tattoos and facial rings. When they got their money, they bought cartons of milk, bread, cheese and crisps from Paddy and went across the road to the picnic tables.

Paddy watched them from his shop. A few were jabbering on mobile phones, others admiring the view. He thought them mediaeval in their look and manner; even their speech was from another age and place, wherever that may be. A couple of mongrel dogs sniffed around the table and they threw them crusts. Three men and two women. Paddy looked at the new names on his register: Cloud Maggs; Sixtop Reeves; Birdie Cole; Zag Homa; Ork Toms. He noted they were all of 'no fixed abode' and pursed his lips, trying to match names with faces. When he peered through the window to jog his memory, they were gone.

He saw them again the following doleday. They came in a battered white van with foreign registration plates, and along with the original five, came four others of similar dress and appearance. Two of the new ones had blue woad on their foreheads, another had a raven on his shoulder. Paddy looked at the new names: Yorrel Hix; Midnight Lyke; Tatan Brown; Filly Downs. They were mannerly and pleasant, pocketed their money and bought bread, sardines, milk, rolling papers, pouches of tobacco, and cans of beans. Then they gathered around the outside tables, talked on phones and had a picnic. Paddy glanced out the window at them, checked the register: his 'family' was growing, twelve regulars and nine irregulars.

George West, a so-so English potter who had settled in the area, came to the shop around midday. He noticed the picnickers and whispered to Paddy, "I yam an ol' hippie, but I never did see the likes of these in my travels. They're like something from a bad trip, man."

Paddy added up his bill, glanced out the window.

"It takes all types to make a world, George, and their likes have to be in it too."

"They're campin' down by the lake at Collock's Shore."

"Easily known they're not locals."

The strangers came to the shop every few days. Paddy thought they didn't wash and smelled of musty hay. He couldn't place their accents or the language they spoke amongst themselves:

"Hey Zag, banda suko Tatan hagur zonka."

"Ah no man, nishin suko zonka."

"Why not? Burka lato sut?"

"Nah. Ishto."

"Hi, two packs a Golden Virginia and four pints a milk."

They all had a similarity in their leather jerkins, muddied jeans and badly-cut hair. It was difficult to tell one from the other and Paddy felt their numbers had grown. George the potter confirmed this when he came to do the Lotto at the weekend.

"Jesus man, there's three vans down at the lake now and a horse-drawn wagon. There must be a couple a dozen of 'em there. There's kids an' all runnin' naked around the place, man."

On dole day Paddy had thirty-eight strangers on the register, an all-time record when he added his regulars. They swarmed outside the shop and blocked the light coming through the door and window.

When they moved to the picnic tables, Paddy sprayed the space with air freshener. He was annoyed at the amount of extra work they generated: all the counting and doling of piles of money, the watching in case they shoplifted. But they also bought a good deal and for this he was pleased.

Before leaving for HQ, the policemen came to see him and buy cigarettes.

"An odd bunch," Sergeant McGee said.

"There's no harm in them though," Paddy suggested, wringing his hands.

"No, no. We believe they're part of some pagan outfit or cult or something."

"Is that so?"

"Earth magic and that sort of thing," Constable Collins said.

"They'd learn plenty about it, if they went cutting hay or footing turf for a few days," Paddy muttered.

"And there's more of them on the way," the sergeant told him.

"I s'pose it can't be helped."

"We're expecting about forty more next week."

"Jesus, that'll be nearly eighty of them so," Paddy winced.

"It's a changing country," Constable Collins sighed.

"There's six helicopters in Ballyjames," the sergeant said. "Every builder has one, and those who don't, have race horses. Solve that one."

"Everyone has a helicopter now." Collins said. "On Sunday they come to Mass in them and land in the football field."

"Terrible fucking noise," McGee said, "you're lucky there's no helicopters around here, Paddy."

"Tis something to be grateful for," agreed Paddy.

Later that evening, a convoy of five vehicles came through Logra. An old school bus painted purple led, followed by a pickup truck with a makeshift cabin in the back. An ambulance towed a grey station wagon and they were tailed by a black Ford cargo van. Paddy watched from the doorway as they passed slowly, laden down with people and gear.

Next morning three horse-drawn wagons with green canvas barrel tops were stopped outside when he opened the shop and he was reminded of a scene from a cowboy film. A woman approached, followed by a toddler. They were scrawny and wild looking. Forest people, thought Paddy, smelling the moss and the leaves from them. She bought two pints of milk and two cans of sardines and paid in small coins.

After she left, two young men arrived, one of them leading a large blonde cat-like animal on a leash. It's a fucking lion, thought Paddy in alarm, stepping back from the counter. The men rattled away in their own lingo:

"Hanz, serto von puka?"

"Ishna zee, sunto zog."

"Cool. Albu onxa."

Paddy heard the animal snarl and curled his toes. The man tightened the leash and spoke firmly to the creature.

"Smells another cat," he said to Paddy, "two cans of beans and a pack of Golden Virginia, please."

He was ten pence short, but Paddy nodded and suffered the loss, relieved to see them leave.

Hardly a day passed without a few wagons going by. Some of them stopped for milk, beans or tobacco. The potter told him a village had sprung up at Collock's Bay, a hive of tents and wagons and vans. They had bonfires nightly and he had heard them singing til dawn, banging and blowing weird instruments.

On doleday their numbers overwhelmed Paddy and he asked two of his regulars to stand by the grocery counter and regulate the queue, letting in only five at a time When the dole-out was finished, Paddy was shattered and he bolted the door and invited his helpers into the kitchen for a drink. He poured a round of whiskey and said,

"It wouldn't be too bad but for the animals. The animals are dangerous. Can you imagine if one of these dogs and a lion or something got into a tiff outside there?"

"You'll have to stop animals coming in," advised Mike McGough, "otherwise they could maul someone."

"It's one of us they'd maul," said Paddy, topping up the tumblers. Matty Hynes nodded,

"I think...I think they're from acircus or something. I don't think they're pagans."

"The pagan might be a bit cleaner alright," ventured McGough.

"I believe Collock's Bay is worse than hell," Paddy said. "George the potter says there's all sort of carry-on down there. Bonfires, sex, drugs, rock and roll."

"I came across one of them in Fogarty's wood," Hynes said, "rooting for pig-nuts he was."

"Pig-nuts will drive them gaga," Paddy sighed, "I'm afraid,

there's now one hundred and forty of them, not including children, in this parish and we're outnumbered by five to one."

"And what the hell is bringin' 'em here?" Hynes asked.

"Because we're a soft touch," Paddy said. "And the cops are more concerned that everyone in Ballyjames has a helicopter than shunting these lunatics to England or Europe, to somewhere that can afford them."

George was pale when he came to the shop. His forehead was furrowed and his eyes were dark and watery.

"I can't sleep. I'm missin' four chickens, man," he said, "and I swear these dudes snatched them."

"That's bad news," Paddy said, "I'm sure the fuckers are nicking stuff from me too."

"I'm afraid to leave the house man, the woods are infested with them. They're weird, man. I think they're all tripped-out. You know what one of 'em told me? He said they were waiting for a spaceship to land on the fuckin' lake."

"You're shittin' me," said Paddy.

"No man, that's what the guy said, they were waiting for a spaceship."

"They're stone cracked."

The strangers bought all the tobacco and all the canned food that Paddy had—sardines, beans, corned beef, steak and kidney pie, beans, peas, and peaches. They cleaned him out of bread and milk and he had deliveries every second day rather than once a week. He smiled to himself, raking in the money he had doled out on behalf of the government a few days before. He wondered if he should order another load of rice and a few more boxes of cigarette rolling papers. And candles.

A couple of miles west of Logra there was a motor accident when a tractor and silage-cutting machine came around a bend and hit a bus of earth people. There were no casualties but the wrecks blocked the road for a day. When the scene was cleared, forty wagons came through in a queue, hooting at every bend, as the policemen had advised. Paddy heard them coming from miles away, honking like Canadian geese. He watched the convoy pass by his door. "Good God," he muttered.

Battered vans with luggage and stuff tied on top, small trucks, cargo wagons, cars with trailers, and cars with boxes on the roofs. All painted odd colours, some multi-coloured. Behind them, a flock of sheep and goats was shepherded by men on piebald ponies. Paddy twitched and went inside.

Before doleday, Paddy got a big delivery from Price-Slash Cash & Carry and restocked the shelves. He got a few new items—noodles, curry powder, tins of tomatoes, pasta and bananas. Around sunset, a drunk with a guitar arrived, and began to sing outside the shop. His voice was mournful and the guitar went blur-blur, blur-blur, rooted in the same chord. The song concerned a maiden's love for a sailor, who had a wife in another port. Paddy banged on the shop window and the performance stopped. What the fuck is he doing here, Paddy wondered.

The drunk muttered to himself and staggered across the road to the picnic tables where he resumed singing. A different song, this one was about an outlaw. He used the back of the guitar as a drum and Paddy put his hands over his ears and waddled into the kitchen. He wondered how long it was since Goldi visited and backtracked through weeks in his head. It was four weeks since he saw her, and so she was due any day soon. He rubbed his hands together, checked the drinks cabinet in the kitchen and turned on the radio.

That night he laboured over the kitchen table, making a big sign from white cardboard. He wrote in block letters:

NO ANIMALS ALLOWED INSIDE.

ONLY FIVE PEOPLE AT A TIME.

PHOTO ID REQUIRED.

He was going to be ready for them. He had arranged for young Martha Fitzpatrick to man the grocery counter while he handled the dole-out. McGough and Hynes would guard the door like the previous week.

Outside he heard the drunk sing again. Other voices were joining in. Paddy peeped through the shop window and saw a chip van parked near the picnic tables. What the hell is happening, he thought. A woman hung a menu board—Chips: 1 *fedro*; Burgers: 2 *fedro*; Chicken Leg: 3 *fedro*; Beans: 1 *fedro*. A man washed potatoes and the drunken singer smoked a cigarette and watched him.

Paddy slept badly, awakened several times by the sound of vehicles maneuvering outside. Occasionally he heard the drunk strum the guitar and sing a song, which petered out after a verse or two. Before dawn, he smelled frying from the chip-van across the road. He lay on his back listening to the sizzle, heard a radio somewhere blare out hit songs and traffic reports. What the heck is going on here, he wondered, what are these people doing here?

Paddy ate a quick breakfast of boiled egg, tea and toast, then washed his hands and opened the front door. He peered around and saw a man in a kilt setting up a canvas-canopied stall near the chip van. A couple dressed in denim assembled a counter beside a battered bread van. Paddy stepped inside and bolted the door. There's something different about today, he thought, wringing his hands. He waited for the police to bring the dole money and hoped his helpers would come soon.

McGough was first to arrive. He told Paddy there were droves and droves of strangers walking the road.

"They're like something out of 'Lord of the Rings'," he said.

Martha Fitzpatrick and Mattie Hynes showed up together and when Paddy opened the door for them, he gasped at the crowd swarming outside.

"There's two crackpots juggling flaming sticks down the road," Martha said, "and there's a fella sellin' cider from the back of a van out there and someone else floggin' cans a beer."

"Oh fuck," shivered Paddy, "this could get outa hand...this fuckin' thing could explode."

Heavy knocking on the front door: cops with the money. Paddy opened the door and Sergeant McGee slipped in with a big black metal box.

"It's shagging mayhem out there," he said, "there's all sorts weirdoes milling around. I told Collins to notify HQ and ask for another car with some of the heavy lads."

"Good thinking," muttered Paddy.

He opened the box behind the counter, counted the money until he lost track and had to begin again. He checked the amount twice and signed the docket for McGee.

"I was thinking," said the sergeant, "it might be a good idea if I stood here near the door...just in case."

"Fine, fine," said Paddy, "Mattie and McGough are givin' a hand too."

A clock chimed ten and the helpers emerged from the kitchen. Paddy nodded and Hynes opened the front door and fixed the large sign overhead:

NO ANIMALS ALLOWED INSIDE.

ONLY FIVE PEOPLE AT A TIME.

PHOTO ID REQUIRED.

Then he tapped the sign and addressed the gawking crowd.

"By order of the Government. Please proceed in an orderly fashion and have your ID ready before you enter."

The crowd mumbled and buzzed like bees. Paddy peered through the window and thought they were getting agitated. They got louder and women directed swear words at the post office. But nobody approached or came to collect their dole.

"What the fuck is up with them?" Paddy asked.

"They're planning something," the sergeant said.

The local recipients arrived in fives and complained about the smell from the strangers, suggesting that many of them were spaced out.

"There's a van out there selling bottles of stuff called fairy juice," James Mills said, "and it's going like hot cakes."

"They're all nuts," Andy Dolan muttered, "wan of 'em is ridin' around on a camel and a lady following him on a shaggin' ostrich."

"I hope they don't settle here," a hippy woman called Starlight said, "they're on a really disturbing frequency."

Paddy doled out money and peeped through the window. A guy with long grey hair and red cape was addressing the crowd in their own cant and Paddy shook his head and turned back to the counter.

Sergeant McGee stepped outside to estimate the size of the crowd. Two, maybe three hundred. Aliens, he thought, they can only be aliens. This crap about the spaceship might be true. These nuts could kidnap us all if we piss them off...could take us back to some other planet. We might need a chopper. A chimp-like child shouted at him and he went back inside.

"A weird bunch," he muttered, "I don't know how they ever got on the Register to draw dole."

The crowd started to chant something like Taba Shoo Taba Shoo! The grey-haired man with the red cape approached the post office, accompanied by two leather-clad men with black helmets and large dog-like animals on leads.

"At ease," the sergeant whispered to Paddy and his staff, "everyone stay calm." His walkie-talkie crackled; reinforcements had arrived. The deputation stopped outside the door and the man in the cape tapped at the notice.

"You are infringing on our rights by these demands!" he shouted into the office. "We cannot be separated from our animals because we are bonded to them. It is written in our constitution. Neither can we be separated from our being in the form of photographs. It is written in our constitution."

"I don't give a shit where it's written," flared Paddy, "but there's no fuckin' animals coming under my roof."

The man relayed Paddy's outburst to the crowd and they booed. Martha got nervous and lit a cigarette. Hynes and McGough lit up too and Paddy coughed, fanning smoke away.

"Jesus Christ," he moaned, "we're bad enough without the fuckin' smoke."

"Let me handle this, Paddy," the sergeant said.

Sergeant McGee stepped outside and spoke to the man with the red cape. It was an intense talk, and eventually the man nodded and shook his hand. Then McGee announced,

"Please line up in alphabetical order."

The man with the cape tipped him on the arm and asked,

"Our alphabet or your alphabet?"

He looked into McGee's eyes and the sergeant felt a jolt go down his legs and bolt him to the ground. He couldn't move his feet, it was like they were embedded in concrete. These are definitely aliens, he thought, and they have us by the balls.

"Your alphabet of course," he replied and sprung back inside. He looked shaken and his eyes rolled as if he was drunk. "Jesus," he muttered, "the smell off them would knock a horse."

Mattie Hynes got him a chair and Paddy asked,

"What the hell are you tryin' to do?"

"Get rid of them, for God's sake. Give them the fuckin' money. Don't piss them off Paddy, we haven't the resources to handle the situation if things go belly up."

Outside a long line was forming in a series of hairpins. There were lots of animals, birds and reptiles. A woman had two snakes, one around her waist and another draped across her shoulders. A half-naked man had a small crocodile on a leash. Paddy bounced in his chair.

"This is ridiculous," he piped, "I can't handle this. There's no animals comin' in here and that's fuckin' that." Martha lit a cigarette and he ordered, "Smoke that fuckin' thing out the back!"

"Cool it Paddy," soothed Hynes, "take it handy."

Martha left the shop and went into the kitchen, closing the door with a heavy thump. A few seconds later they heard her scream and she came running back.

"There's a tiger or something in the toilet!"

Paddy swore and jumped from the seat. Hynes closed the kitchen door firmly and McGee gave Martha his chair. McGough opened a bottle of orangeade and passed it to her.

"It was drinking water outa the bowl...it was huge...big as a calf."

"Sweet mother of Jesus," blessed Paddy.

Sergeant McGee spoke to Constable Collins on the walkie-talkie and requested lawmen be sent to the post office.

"The lads have machine guns," he told Paddy, "let there be no panic. And we have a chopper on alert, just in case."

"Panic?" echoed Paddy, "no panic and we surrounded by weirdoes who're making a fuckin' open zoo out of my house. And you say let there be no panic? And now a few lads with machine guns are joining us. And you have a fucking chopper hovering over my house like a wasp. I don't know what this fuckin' country is becoming."

"Paddy, Paddy, Paddy!" pleaded McGough, "Take it aisey."

The man with the red cape tapped on the door, poked his head inside and asked,

"Are we ready?"

Silence.

"Ready?" he asked again, looking at McGee who was staring at his toes.

"Ready for what?" asked Paddy.

"Ready for our money."

"Whose money?"

"The universal money that passes from you to us and back to you again and so on ad infinitum."

Paddy looked at him, and was about to lambaste the leech, when three cops in black tracksuits stormed into the post office, each carrying a briefcase. They huddled around Sergeant McGee, opened their cases and assembled machine guns in a couple of clicks. The man with the red cape backed away from the door and addressed the crowd excitedly.

"First, get that fuckin' tiger in the toilet," Paddy shouted to the machine gun cops.

"Don't go too near him," McGee advised, opening the kitchen door for them.

They slipped inside, guns poised, finger on the trigger. Paddy waited, McGee watched the back of their heads through the slightly open door. Martha closed her eyes, covered her ears and waited for the shots. Hynes and McGough stayed near the front door in case of emergency. The hunters returned minutes later and muttered.

"Clean, nothing there."

"I definitely saw it," Martha said. "Would it be gone upstairs?"

"Up-fucking where?" cried Paddy, glancing at the ceiling in alarm.

"Best to wait until he comes down," McGee said, "you've no chance when the animal has the higher ground."

"This is fuckin' it!" flared Paddy, "I've fuckin' had it. There's a tiger above on my bed and a lost tribe of weirdoes waitin' outside my house, like it was Noah's fuckin' ark..."

"It's alright Paddy," consoled Mattie Hynes, "everything will be fine. Toughen yourself."

The crowd was quiet, apart from the odd roar or bark of an animal. The busker staggered to a halt near the post office door and began a song about two sisters who loved the same man. Paddy banged on the window and ordered him to move away. He meandered a few steps and started a song about a pirate, which many of the crowd knew and they sang along with him. Paddy stared at the cans of beans and sardines packed on the shelves of the shop, tins of stew, soup and spam, tomatoes, yams. There was also a box of ripe bananas and a barrel of grapes from Greece. He had enough to feed Napoleon's army and if this crowd didn't buy it, no one else would.

"We'll get rid of one problem at a time, Paddy," Sergeant McGee said, "let 'em in without the ID, and stamp their hands or something so they can't impersonate."

"This is ridiculous," Paddy muttered, looking at the list of odd names and the payment for each, "I'll draw the line with the animals...no animals, birds or reptiles. Of any sort. Tell that to the fuckin' Batman with the red cape."

McGee stepped outside. The busker sang a song concerning a mining disaster in Australia; a child beat a drum beside him. The sergeant beckoned to Batman and relayed the postmaster's edict. Paddy watched from inside, saw them having an animated conversation, Batman laying down the law and Sergeant McGee nodding in agreement. They shook hands and McGee returned to the post office.

"That's grand," he said to Paddy, "no animals."

The first five arrived quietly and gave their names to Paddy in low, polite voices. He requested they spell it and he ran his finger down the list of recipients Then he told them to put their right-hand palm down on counter and he postmarked the back of the paw.

The sixth payee, a lanky woman named Inka Rosey, asked Paddy to postmark her forehead rather than the back of her hand. Eyes luminous with fairy juice, she leaned forward and he stamped her to get rid of her. Ungi Tool, the next in line, requested a forehead postmark as well. Excitedly he asked Paddy if he could time date it to the exact second and Paddy lied that he could. Ungi lay down his head and got stamped over the left eye. Then someone asked if they could have a stamp over each eye and the postmaster

71

said that cost a fedro and they paid. It was then Paddy realised that the dolers were leaving without buying anything in the shop. He glanced across to the other counter and saw Martha Fitzpatrick paint her fingernails, protected by a sergeant and three cops with machine guns.

"Hold it!" he shouted before the third batch came in and the office stood still. He beckoned to Sergeant McGee and wondered in a whisper if he might send the gunners on a tea break to thin out the shop.

"They can go into the kitchen," Paddy whispered, "tell them to take their time. Make a drop of tea for themselves."

"What about the tiger?" McGee asked.

"Just keep the door closed."

Without the armed guard, the office was light and airy. Martha stood ready to serve but nobody came to her counter; they all turned on their heels after being postmarked and left the office. Paddy was baffled. He made a sales pitch to recipients while he postmarked them. *"The shop is open if you want anything"* was regular as a mantra until he noticed a cat peeping out of a woman's backpack.

"I said no animals," he chided.

"It's only a little putty-tat," she purred and he stamped her on the back of the hand with undue force.

The mantra began again, but drew no results, nobody shopped. A guy brought in a deerhound but Paddy didn't notice. Someone else came in with an anteater, but he didn't see that either. His brain was buzzing when he got to Fraz Love, a tall slender woman in leopard skin pelt with a snake coiled around her waist. She gave her name,

Paddy found it on the list, told her about the shop as he counted out sixty-five fedros and fifty pence. He picked up his stamper and aimed for the flesh he saw on the counter, recoiling in mid-strike when the snake raised his head. Paddy screamed, fell off the chair. Martha screamed, "A fuckin' shnake bit him! I saw it!"

Ms. Love fled. Sergeant McGee rushed to Paddy, and Mattie Hynes cleared the shop and shut the door without explanation. Hearing the commotion, the cops with guns stormed from the kitchen.

"A shnake bit Paddy," Martha told them, "a woman had him inside her dress."

Paddy moaned on the floor, tears on his cheeks, ignoring the sergeant's questions. "Awww," he moaned, "awww…Jesus Christ… awww a fuckin snake…awww…fuck…awww."

McGough got a glass of brandy and they sat Paddy on the chair, still moaning.

"He's in shock", whispered McGee, "total shock."

After a few sips of brandy he spoke weakly,

"I said no animals, birds or reptiles. Are you fuckin' blind McGough? How the fuck did a snake get into my premises and almost kill me behind my own counter?" McGough blushed, looked at the floor and shrugged.

"Sorry boss," he said, "she had the snake hidden. I didn't see it."

"She had it inside her dress," Martha helped.

"Well," said Paddy, "if they can't play by the rules, they can go and fuck each other, because there's no more dough for them. That's it. Fuck 'em. No man should have to put up with this abuse from leeches and riff-raff from Mars. And the smell of drink and shit from the fuckers. Jesus Christ, I could be in the fuckin' belly of a python if it wasn't for the grace of God. Fuck 'em!"

Paddy trembled and sipped the brandy. The shop was silent. Outside the busker sang about working on the railroad and the crowd joined in the chorus, climaxing in "Poor Paddy's workin' on the railway!"

"Fuck 'em," hissed Paddy. He shook his head and drained the glass, beckoning to McGough for a refill.

"Bringing the snake in was out of order," offered Sergeant McGee.

"There was no need for that," added Hynes, "and they were warned often enough about it."

"I'm sure I've doled three thousand fedro," Paddy said, "and not wan fuckin' cent have they spent in my shop. Not wan fuckin' cent."

"I didn't sell a box a matches," piped Martha.

"They're all buyin' from the traders out there," informed one of the cops.

"That's the thanks I get," muttered Paddy, accepting the second brandy from McGough. "I'm sending the rest of that dole money back with ye to the barracks and they can go there for it. I'm not putting my life in danger for that shower of twerps."

"Jesus Paddy," McGee said quietly, "that could cause all sorts of problems. They could throw that anti-discrimination law at you."

Paddy looked at him, shook his head in disgust and had a swallow of brandy.

"I'm not able for this shit," he muttered.

"Maybe...maybe," began Sergeant McGee, "maybe Batman would give it to them...you know."

"Batman? The nut with the cape? I don't give a rat's tat who gives it to them, but it won't be Paddy. No sir, been there, done that, have the scar. Batman can have the bag of cash and give it to the busker for all I care."

He drank the brandy, sniffled, and glanced out the window at the crowd of misfits. Many had animals, many were unsteady on their feet and laughing hysterically. A woman on an ostrich passed the window and he flinched at the size of the bird, eyes big as duck eggs. He turned away when a trouserless child made faces at him.

Sergeant McGee stepped outside and beckoned to Batman. They spoke for a few minutes, heads nodded and they both returned to the office. Batman bowed before Paddy, mumbling how sorry he was about the snake incident. He would of course distribute the dole to the rest of the tribe, and asked to be allowed postmark them. Paddy begrudgingly passed him an inkpad and stamper, then the bag of cash and list of names. "They've to sign next to their name," Paddy said, "but an X will do to save time."

Batman and his cohorts stood outside the post office and he called out names. A line of communicants weaved toward him and he stamped their foreheads. They signed the government sheet of paper, got their money and dribbled back into the crowd. Some of them were rocky on their feet and a few had to be carried. But all in all, it was a smooth process and Paddy and his helpers watched from the shop.

"Christ," he said, "but isn't it an awful waste, to be handin' out money to that shower of libes."

A drunk staggered towards the shop and they moved away from the door to let him enter. Martha went behind the counter and the customer stood in the middle of the floor and pointed at the shelf over her head. Paddy tried to figure out what he wanted. Figrolls? Custard? Peas? Sugar? Tobacco?

Frustrated, the man waved his arms and tried to talk but failed. He staggered out again and Paddy muttered.

"And fuck you too, mate."

A little later a barefoot woman with green hair bought a pint of milk and a can of beans. That was the final sale of the day.

Sergeant McGee and Batman came back to the post office and Paddy examined the sheet of recipient's names. He signed it and gave it to the policeman who avowed, that all was well that ended well.

"Indeed," Paddy sighed. Batman offered the postmaster his hand and said,

"May you be filled with wine of the gods."

The police waited until the crowd moved away, then took off to HQ with blue lights flashing. Stallholders packed their wares into vans and cars and crows picked through the litter on the road. The busker sat at the picnic table and talked to himself while rolling a cigarette. Paddy locked the shop and settled into the kitchen with his staff. He put two six packs of Guinness on the table, a bottle of whiskey, a large bottle of red lemonade and four tumblers.

"Never in all my born days did I see such weirdos as that crowd," he said, "Christ but I hope I don't have to deal with them everyday."

"And the smell of them," Martha shivered.

"I'm sure they sleep with them fuckin' animals," McGough said.

"I hope they're not settlin' here," Hynes muttered, "they could make a right haimes out of a place...fuckin' cops with machine guns would be livin' in our ears."

"And helicopters looking down on us," added Martha

"They don't give a shit about the cops," Paddy said, opening cans of stout, "the cops are no match for them, guns or no guns. Christ, if they set a few lions or tigers on the cops, what would they do? Hah?"

"And the crocodile...uggg!" added Martha, "He really gave me the creeps."

They drank the six packs and Paddy poured a round a round of whiskey.

"Like," he said, "what happens if a few of them animals get loose and hide in the woods? Hah? Nobody is safe."

"Them fuckin' lions could breed around here," Hynes muttered.

"If that crocodile got into the lake..." Martha shivered.

"This crowd could fuck the whole place up," said Paddy, shaking his head.

A second bottle of whiskey was opened and Mattie Hynes sang *Lovely Leitrim*. Martha told them about a night she went to a nightclub in Dublin with her sister and danced with a man who offered her cocaine. Paddy said the world was gone to hell and now they saw it close up in their own parish. McGough said the place was going downhill since the state joined the Federation. He was drunk and getting emotional, "We have nothin' now. The government sold out. Every fucker is milking us."

After a short silence, Paddy sang an old rebel song from the revolution and they all joined in the chorus. McGough recited a poem with a line that went *We'll all be rooned said Hanrahan, before the year is out.* Paddy collapsed at the table and Martha and Mattie carried him upstairs to bed. McGough gave another poem and Martha sang *You Are My Sunshine.* They finished all Paddy's drink, put off the lights and locked the door.

The road outside was littered with trash and the busker sat at the picnic table singing *Blowin' in the Wind.* Suddenly a huge boom rocked the night. Boom! Boom! Fireworks exploded and the lake lit up with a million stars reflecting from the sky. The waterfall glowed in luminous orange from another blast of fireworks. Cheers rose from the lakeside. Drums beat and instruments blared strident noise. "Oh Christ," said the busker, "they're calling down the spaceship."

For the rest of his life, the busker would tell about the night he saw the UFO descend on Logra Lake and unload hundreds of beings. He would cross his heart, look listeners in the eye and ask, "How could anyone be the same after seeing that?"

There was a party for the newcomers he said, but he wasn't invited. All night they played music like he could never describe because it was definitely from another galaxy. It stopped when the birds began to sing and only then could he sleep at the picnic table.

When he woke up, wagons were driving past at funeral pace and the tribe was on the move. All sorts of vehicles, wagons and contraptions, weighed down with bags, boxes and gadgets. He hailed on many of them to give him a ride but they refused, pointing out that he didn't have a postmark. Even their kids had postmarks now. All day they passed, a long snaking procession that hooted a hundred horns as they approached bends on the road to Mulla. He asked where they were heading and they just said that they were going further.

It was early afternoon when Paddy Petty came to. The daylight was blinding and his head ached. He heard wagons rumbling and rolling past his window and then he remembered the strangers and moaned, "Oh no."

Hung-over and cranky, Paddy boiled an egg and ate it with a slice of toast. A mug of strong black sweet tea brought life to his face and he went to the shop. From the door he watched rigs crawl past, dogs and exotic animals tethered to them. They were leaving. Relief came over him until he thought of the boxes of bananas and grapes on the counter. A lynx lunged at him and he closed the door and watched the procession through the shop window. They were like a disheveled army of some kind; they had a determination about them. Thanks be to God they were leaving; his hangover began to ease. Then some bastard lobbed a dirty nappy at the window and frightened the life out of him.

At four-thirty the mail van came and delivered three pieces of post: a credit card statement for Martha Fitzgerald, something for George the Potter from Amnesty and a postcard from Goldie for himself. *Hi Paddy, hope the summer weather is agreeing with you. I will drop by on Thursday. Look forward to catching up.* That's today, thought Paddy. His mood lifted and he went to the kitchen and made himself a strong Irish coffee. Then the world didn't seem so crazy.

The last motorized vehicle passed around six that evening and then, in a cloud of dust, horses, donkeys, lamas, sheep, mules, cows, yaks and buffalo came, herded by wild youths. One of them flashed the 'F' sign at Paddy and he withdrew from the window.

It was sunset by the time they had all passed. Paddy stared at the amount of trash around his shop and along both sides of the road, in each direction. He'd have to call the county council in the morning. The busker crossed the road towards him.

"They're gone," he said, clicking his fingers, "just like that."

"May God speed them," said Paddy.

"I don't suppose you have any drink for sale…a drop of rum or vodka…I'm drinkin' that fuckin' fairy juice for the past two days and I need to drop anchor."

"No drink. No drink. Mulla is your best bet, fifteen miles down to your right. There's pubs there with plenty drink."

"There won't be much left by the time that crowd have passed through. I saw them down in Kerry and they drank the town of Kenmare dry in two hours. And I mean dry, down to the cooking wine in the supermarkets."

"I have to close the shop now."

"That's alright, I don't mind. You do what you have to do and don't mind me."

Paddy sighed and shut the door, banged bolts into place and turned the key in a creaky lock. Fairy juice and Earth People, crocodiles and ostriches, singers and machine-guns, choppers and snakes—he had a lot to tell Goldie about when she arrived. The busker began to wail about knock, knock, knocking on Heaven's door. Paddy sighed and went to the kitchen to make another Irish coffee. He was almost there.

Harry's Karma

Harry Olbert was a wealthy man, like his father and grandfather before him. Importers of timber and exporters of livestock since the days of the sailing ships, the family had talent for making money and keeping ahead of the times. In Harry's era, they expanded and diversified, becoming Irish distributors for a number of European gourmet food companies. He converted Olbert's old derelict waterfront property into shops and apartments, and that made him another fortune. Then he went into semi-retirement and let his son Frank run the organization.

Robust and reserved, Harry had a healthy head of white backswept hair, a strong forehead and heavy dark-rimmed spectacles.

Almost seventy, he'd been a widower fifteen years and had reverted to a bachelor lifestyle. He was fit for his age and dressed smart, in tweed jacket, cord trousers, plain shirt and striped tie. Harry drove a small silver Mercedes and lived alone in Glebe House, a Georgian mansion that overlooked the estuary and was hidden from the town by a shoulder of trees.

Harry had been an accidental businessman. A good pianist and in his youth, he had notions of becoming a jazz musician. Back then he fancied himself living in the great cities of Europe, having coffee with Picasso and gelato with Fellini. He got as far as London when his brother Nigel was killed in a car crash and Harry came back home to help in the family business. It was only to be for a while, and then he met Hilda Hamilton. They talked poetry and music and he fell in love, even though something about Hilda unsettled his soul. She was different to the other women he knew. High-spirited, passionate, and flamboyant, she could create a scene in a blink. Like the night she stormed from Lady Campbell's ball, when the Lancaster sisters waved at Harry. He could have married Lily Lancaster. Maybe he should have. She bore her husband four sons and two daughters. He read it in her obituary. He thought about her more often than he thought about Hilda.

Beautiful and dreamy in their wedding album, Hilda Olbert had a breakdown on the second birthday of her only child, Frank. After that there was little relief: she was sporadically plagued by saints and demons, especially Lucifer, who had a girlfriend in the cellar. Their marriage was traumatic and Hilda spent much of it in exclusive psychiatric hospitals named after obscure saints.

"We have everything and yet we have nothing," Harry used say to close friends. There was no arty sojourn in Paris or Barcelona, no hanging out in Greenwich Village or pilgrimage to Majorca to meet Robert Graves. Harry made business trips instead, and played the piano at home alone.

Nowadays he listened more than he played, and had eclectic tastes: Glenn Miller; Irish parlor classics; Charlie Parker; The Chieftains; Mary Coughlan; Maria Callas; Martin Hayes. He was a founding member of the local musical society and bankrolled the annual opera. It was his social platform, and a few years after Hilda died, he had a romance with the singer Bella Rourke, when she came to perform in the *Pirates of Penzance*. It shocked the town but everyone said he was entitled to a flutter. A short, sweet and discreet relationship, it alarmed his son Frank that the old hog could still go rooting.

The following year, the society performed *Spanish Ladies* and the exotic Louisa Garcia tangoed with Harry. The year after, it was Molly Seacomb from *Fiddler on the Roof*. In the library at Glebe House, Harry kept the programs from old shows, occasionally browsed through them, recalling lovers, reliving love. The past few seasons had been barren and he wondered if he was over the hill.

Harry sat on the audition board when the musical society were casting for *Raggle Taggle Gypsies*. That was the first time he saw Mandy Hailey, who auditioned for the role of Little Nancy. In her early thirties, she was petite with a shy face and dark hair, just short of her shoulders. Though she looked the part, they felt her voice didn't suit. She was disappointed and asked if she could play violin in the orchestra. The board listened to her perform, and while she hadn't great talent, they agreed she had enthusiasm and let her in to boost the strings and add color to the pit.

The society rehearsed in the town hall and sometimes Harry dropped by and stood at the back of the balcony. He always applauded when they finished and shouted 'Bravo! Bravo!' Occasionally he invited the team to Haran's Hotel for refreshments and treated them lavishly. Sometimes a singsong caught fire and became a party. Great nights, especially when Harry whipped off his jacket and sat at the piano. One night he hammered out *When I'm Sixty-Four* and they clapped and cheered and he sweated like a rock star and drank a gin and tonic to come down from the clouds. Mandy Hailey came to him and said, "Wow! That was fantastic!"

She sparked something in him and over the following weeks, a friendship developed between them. He heard she was new to the area and finding it difficult to get to know people. Divorced with two children, she was studying to be a lawyer and had a year to finals. Harry thought her cute, and loved how she tilted her head while she talked. Her voice was polite and hinted of the country, but he didn't think her a farmer's daughter; more likely she came from a horse-breeding family. He wondered if they might become romantic, considering their age difference.

Mid-way through rehearsals, Mandy told Harry that she found the scores difficult and was considering quitting the orchestra. The news alarmed him and he offered to tutor her to bring her up to speed. Next afternoon she came to Glebe House and they went through the pieces. It was laborious and he thought her more interested in chatting than learning. They had tea in the library by a log fire and Mandy said, "Thanks Harry, I think I'll get the hang of it."

They practiced twice a week and *The Gypsy March*, *Nell and Sally* and so on thumped through the manse. Mandy always had tea and was hesitant to leave. Glebe House enchanted her with its high ceilings and tall windows, the old oil paintings on the wall and the maritime antiques in the hall, the stillness and the calmness of the great rooms and the views of the estuary and the ocean beyond. Her scent lingered long after she'd left and Harry savored it, singing arias to his dreams.

Days before *Raggle Taggle* was due to open, Mandy arrived to Glebe House unannounced. She was distressed, and told Harry that her mother had taken ill while on a visit to London and she had to go there immediately. He asked if he could help in any way and she said, "I hate to admit this, but I'm a little tight for money…"

"Would five hundred be enough?"

He wrote her a check and she hugged him and whispered,

"That's great. You're an angel Harry."

Apart from Harry Olbert, nobody really missed Mandy from *Raggle Taggle Gypsies*. She wasn't there for opening night and the whole performance was an anti-climax for him. He didn't enjoy the post-show bash and left without doing a party piece. She returned a week after the musical closed and Harry fussed around her when she visited Glebe House. They had tea in the library and he told her about the performance and how she was missed from it.

"It was flat!" he exclaimed, "I could only take one night." Mandy smiled and hugged her knees.

"Oh it's great to be back, Harry. And thanks for your help, it made a great difference to Mum that I was there for her."

She said she'd just started work in a law office and wondered if the loan repayment could be put off until she got settled in. Harry said certainly and she fawned,

"God Harry, I don't know what I'd do without you."

Mandy visited him once or twice every week, occasionally with her children. Shelia and Sean were four and six and though they annoyed Harry with their constant bickering and clinging to their mother, he always gave them money for chocolate. He asked her advice on the house and installed a dishwasher as she suggested. On fine days they pottered in the garden and Harry felt decades younger, watching her bend over and plant seedlings.

She made dinner at Glebe House on Easter Saturday night and her cooking was so fine, it surprised Harry: he put it down to good breeding and she went higher in his estimation. They had ginger pears and cream by the fire in the sitting room and talked about the strangeness of life, trading tit-bits from their marriages. Harry showed her photos of Hilda; Mandy broke down telling how she was abandoned for another woman. He dried her tears and held her in his arms.

"I'd better get back," she sighed, "I forgot about the baby-sitter."

Frank Olbert's office overlooked the harbour, and he stared out the window and into deep grey water while his wife Orla related the local gossip: a young woman was regularly seen visiting Glebe House. She had also heard a joke in the supermarket about Harry's china doll.

"There's no fool like an old fool," she said. "You have to talk to him."

After a week of nagging from Orla, Frank took his father to lunch on the pretence of a business chat. Bald and Buddhist, Frank was tall and nervous like his mother, and he sometimes had her stammer. He carried a small photo of her in the breast pocket of his jacket for protection. While Harry stared blankly at a spreadsheet, Frank leaned forward and said, "By the way, what's going on between you and that lady?"

"What lady?"

"That...that lay-lady who visits you."

"She's just a friend."

"Be...be careful."

"She's a lawyer."

"Be extra careful."

After a short consultation back at the office, Frank and Orla decided to contact a private investigator.

Mandy came to Glebe House for Saturday night supper and Harry thought her anxious. When he asked if something was bothering her, she said her ex-husband had suddenly turned up and rented a flat nearby.

"Good God," muttered Harry

"He's seeking more access to the children. Lucky I work in a law office," she said with an ironic laugh.

Harry nodded, topped up her wine. "Don't worry," he said, "You're doing great. Be sure to let me know if things get hairy."

"Thank you Harry," she whispered, "you're a very good friend."

She worried that she wasn't able to see him as often as she liked. Work was hectic and most nights she was studying. Plus the car was unreliable. She was on the lookout for a new one; that would free her up a bit more.

"Anyway, I'd better get back and let the babysitter home."

Harry hugged her goodnight in the hall and gave her a gentleman's kiss on the cheek.

Olberts were offered the Irish agency for Arbano coffee on the same day that Frank heard from the private investigator. He was a bundle of nerves and went to meditate in the boardroom. Orla took control and after an hour of hard thinking, she called Harry and asked that he take an interest in the Arbano opportunity.

"You know more about coffee than anyone," she said, "and you love Italy."

Hearing strain in her voice, Harry got wary but played along. He asked a few financial questions and wondered about demographics. Orla brought samples to Glebe House and later, Harry and Mandy tasted them and judged them to be haute-cafe. Next morning he called the office and spoke to his daughter-in-law.

"Excellent coffee," he said, "I was particularly impressed by their espresso. With the interest here for cappuccinos, lattes and God knows what, I'd say we have a winner."

"Good," she said, "they're anxious to get moving on the deal. Fancy a few days in Italy?"

"Sure," he laughed and Orla booked himself and Frank on a flight to Milan to meet the Arbano family.

Harry spoke Italian reasonably well and did most of the negotiating. Frank threw in occasional comments and wrote the fine print to a deal that made everyone happy. To celebrate, Don Arbano took them to Vito's for dinner and Harry ended the night waltzing with a countess on a marble floor.

While in Italy, Frank had planned a serious conversation with his father about Mandy Hailey. Orla and himself had role-played the scene several times in the office. Frank would be firm and lay it on the line that the woman was trouble...but he kept putting it off. Things keep getting in the way, he told Orla on the phone. Do it, she ordered. Finally, on the plane home Frank said to Harry, "I have news for you. She's not a lawyer, you know."

"What? Who?"

"The Hailey lady. She's not a lawyer, she's a cook."

"What are you talking about?"

"The lay...lay...lady who calls to you, she was a cook in Harold's Restaurant in Kellystown. They hey-hey fired her."

"Where did you hear that bullshit?"

"Somebody told Orla."

Harry opened his mouth to reply but didn't. His face paled and he sat back into the seat, lips quivering.

Soon as he arrived home, Harry Olbert called Jonathan Harold and asked about Mandy Hailey. A great cook, he heard, but a pathological liar. Before she worked at Harold's, herself and the husband had a restaurant in Ballycrawford called Sizzle. Dozens of diners were defrauded in a credit card scam and the husband got jail. Harry stilled.

"Are you sure it's the same woman?" he asked incredulously.

"Does she drive a black Ford Escort with a dent on the bonnet?"

"She does," Harry replied.

After the call he sat down and fumed like an overheated engine. Sweat pimpled his forehead and his glasses steamed up. What the hell is she at? He thought to phone her. No, better confront her in person. All that day and night his heart thumped and he walked in and out of empty rooms in Glebe House, just like the way he walked around on the night Hilda went into labor.

Mandy phoned to welcome him home from Italy but he couldn't talk to her. His breathing got faster and he made the excuse that he had visitors and ended the call abruptly. Next morning she rang again and he said he was just leaving the house and would speak to her later. He went downtown and bought a call monitor. He thought about asking his lawyer to write to her at work and demand immediate repayment of the loan. That would shake her. What was the name of the law firm? Foster & Gallen? Frost & Mallan? He couldn't remember. She said it was someplace up north. It would come to him.

She phoned several times over the following fortnight, but

Harry didn't answer. When she drove up the avenue he went to the bathroom and stayed there until he heard her car turn in the gravel and leave. Eventually she stopped calling and Glebe House became quiet. Harry's routine returned: a spot of gardening on fine days, lunch at the hotel, afternoon nap; a couple of hours watching television after tea; walk on the strand on Sunday.

Though he vowed never again to let Mandy inside his house, she slipped into his mind every now and then, and he couldn't stop her. One night while drinking alone at home, he was tempted to phone her, just for a chat. Maybe, he reasoned—maybe the scam was all her husband's doing and she was an unwitting associate. Maybe everyone's wrong about her. Worse case scenario, she's a classic poacher turned gamekeeper.

After a while she was in his mind before he woke in the morning and sat there all day. He lost interest in the garden and moped around Glebe House, expecting his phone to ring, waiting for her car to come up the drive. It took great will power not to call her and he was glad of the distraction when the Arbano people came over to launch the coffee in Ireland. They played golf, went to a mediaeval banquet, sang arias late at night in the hotel. He was sick for a week after they left.

The investigator reported Mandy hadn't visited Harry in over two months and that her husband had moved in with her. Orla and Frank high-fived each other and booked a week's holiday in Vitalis Spa. The day they left, Harry was playing the piano in Glebe House when the doorbell chimed. It was Mandy and he was rattled for words.

"Hello stranger," she greeted, "I thought you had emigrated on me."

She looked pretty in a short denim skirt and black tights and invited herself inside.

"I got you a little something in Dublin when I was at the High Court."

She handed him a small gift and he opened it standing in the hall. A CD of Bing Crosby's greatest recordings.

"Thanks very much Mandy. I don't know what to say."

Beads of sweat dimpled his nose as she chattered that it was great to see him and how well he looked.

Harry made two martinis in the sitting room and she did most of the talking. Work was going well and a suitable arrangement had been made with her husband in regards to the children. Of course her car was on its last legs but otherwise, life was good. Harry nodded, smiled, and peeped over the top of his glasses. He thought to hint about the stories he'd heard, but shuffled the notion to the back of his mind for the moment. She hugged her knees and he smiled and made two more martinis. "And how have you been Harry? I really missed seeing you."

"Oh I've been busy, busy."

"We could both do with a night out."

The Boathouse was Harry's favorite hideaway. Down the coast about twenty miles, it was a quiet, discreet eatery with eight tables and an expensive menu. Mandy said it felt real romantic and glanced around the room to see who else was there; she didn't recognize anybody. He suggested the Beef Wellington for two and ordered a bottle of Chateaux de Roche. They had lobster salad and champagne to start and Harry felt life in his groins for the first time in years.

While Frank and Orla were away, Harry and Mandy saw each other daily. They dined out and drank brandy and champagne, smoked cigars and whispered to each other like new lovers. One night she was too drunk to drive home from Glebe House and had to sleep in the guest room. Harry lay awake wondering if the time was yet right to be more intimate. He no longer thought about the stories he'd heard—or the money he was owed—but hungered instead for the warmth of her body. He began to conjure up exotic places where they might experience unfettered romance. He saw Mandy and himself in Hawaiian shirts and shorts, walking on a deserted white beach at sunset. Dining under the moon, palm trees, mellow candles and smooth wine. The next time she visited he said, "I'm thinking about going on a holiday. South Seas...Fiji maybe...would you consider coming along?"

"Ah Harry! That's a lovely idea."

"I'll take care of the cost."

"You're so good. I'd love to but it would be difficult with work and the kids. And I have to try and put a bit of money aside for a new car."

Seeing disappointment on his face, she added,

"But maybe we could go somewhere for a weekend."

Mandy saw a car she liked and asked Harry if he'd check it out with her. They drove to the showroom in his Mercedes, and she wore a grey pin-stripe suit and carried a slim black briefcase. The car was a silver Honda station wagon with low mileage and priced eight grand. Harry thought it good value and it handled well during the test drive. But he felt it didn't suit her: it was too big or something and she looked like a pixie behind the wheel. "Think over it for a day or two," he suggested.

"Shouldn't I start the loan process anyway, just in case?"

"I suppose it can do no harm."

That night she cooked dinner in Glebe House and he dusted off a bottle of vintage wine. She spoke about work and some of the interesting cases she was dealing with.

"Who do you work with again?"

"Harris & Finch. Did I not give you my card?"

"I don't think so."

She searched in her briefcase for a business card, but couldn't find any. Shrugged and said,

"So you think the Honda is a good deal, Harry?"

Diplomatic as he could be, he tried to talk her away from the car. She looked dreamily at him as he spoke and he knew her mind was made up.

"If I got a bank loan, could you go guarantor for me?" she asked.

Harry frowned, had a sip of wine. The old stories churned in his head. She already owed him five hundred pounds and there was no talk of repayment.

"I'm sure we could work something out," he said.

"Ah Harry, you're great."

They moved into the sitting room to watch a Woody Allen movie on TV. It bored Harry and he drank to pass the time. Mandy snuggled against him on the couch and when the film was over she whispered,

"The reason I want a new car so badly is that I have a recurring nightmare of my ex driving into the river with the kids in my old banger. Does that make any sense to you Harry?"

He wrapped his arms around her and she snuggled closer.

"I feel safe with you, Harry," she whispered.

He kissed her on the head and she turned her face to meet his lips.

Harry kissed her up the stairs and into his bedroom. She moaned when his hands crept under her blouse and they lay back on the bed. Passionate and hot, Harry faltered in the final lap. He couldn't couple and after a few attempts, gave up. They slept back-to-back and she was first up in the morning and brought him coffee in bed.

"Thanks for taking care of me," she said.

"I can do better."

"You were great."

After she left, Harry relived the night, touch by touch. It bothered him that he was not able to make love. Would she mention to anyone that life force had left him? Was it a sign of death, he wondered, or was it just lack of practice? He hadn't slept with a woman for nearly five years.

Harry took Mandy to Kinsale for a gourmet weekend and though they dined and danced like newlyweds, there was little magic in the bedroom. Awake till dawn with fears of impotency, Harry aged ten years in two nights. Returning home he apologized for his lack of spirit, joking that he wasn't as young as he thought. There was resigned sadness in his voice and Mandy rubbed his knee and said not to worry, it was enough for her to be with him. Anyway, if he wanted, his condition could be helped by medication. There were all sorts of drugs for that now, she told him.

"Christ, I can't walk into Doc Hogan and tell him I want medicine to help me perform. I don't want anyone to know my business."

"Maybe I could get it for you. A good friend of mine is a doctor in Dublin."

The weather changed next day and Harry felt low and lonely, pestered by something beyond his grasp. He wandered aimlessly around Glebe House, haunted by memories of Hilda. Outside the beech leaves were curling into gold and undertaker crows walked the lawn, cawing autumnal mantras. Harry was thinking about a holiday in the sun with Mandy when his bank manager phoned.

"Mr. Olbert, we noticed you signed a letter of guarantee for a loan application by a Ms. Mandy Hailey. As you are a valued client of the bank, I should tell you that we're concerned. Ms. Hailey has serious credit problems."

Harry eased into a chair.

"There's some mistake here Tom, I never signed anything. I mean, I know the lady...but no, no, I never signed any forms for a loan."

"Well someone does a remarkably good impression of your signature, Mr. Olbert."

"I don't know anything about this Tom."

"The bank will take the appropriate action in that case, Mr. Olbert. In light of this, you might want to examine your checking account and bring any irregularities to my attention."

"Thank you Tom."

That evening, Harry was reading 'Seven Secrets of the Samurai' in the library when Mandy came around. She was dressed in a tight ruby skirt and a pale blouse that showed modest cleavage. Displaying a big bunch of flowers and a bag of groceries, she announced that she'd be cooking him dinner, they'd cause to celebrate. She brought the groceries into the kitchen and arranged the flowers in two vases. Then she hugged Harry and whispered.

"Can we have a drink please? I've great news."

"Sure. Let's go to the sitting-room."

She sat on the couch and Harry made martinis. He would let her get comfortable with a couple of drinks and then confront her. He had the script in his head: Mandy, you've been playing games with me. There's no such law firm as Harris & Finch in this country. You're not a law student, you're an unemployed cook. You've forged my signature...

"I'm going to buy the Honda," she said, "I put a deposit on it. I'm meeting my bank manager in the morning. So, fingers crossed."

"Indeed."

"And! My friend sent me the medicine for you."

Harry's mind changed script. Maybe he could mix business and pleasure. Stave off the execution. Play her game. Let the bank manager wield the hatchet, the morning after. She took a little bottle from her handbag and handed it to him.

The label on the container read: Take one as required. Harry peered at the pills and wondered how they worked. Would they affect his heart? What would a samurai do?

"It's OK to take them with a drink or two," Mandy said.

He unscrewed the cap and spilled a few into his palm. They looked like purple M & M's and reminded him of the Nins that Doctor Hogan used give his late wife when she needed sedation.

"And Harry, I was thinking, now that my car problem is sorted, maybe we could go on that holiday. It would be nice to spend Christmas in the sun."

He peered closer at the tiny writing on the pills: WIN. Or was it NIN? His sight blurred and his hands trembled. He stared at Mandy and awkwardly rose from the armchair.

"Go away," he gasped, "Get out..."

"Harry! What's wrong Harry?"

She was distracted by noise outside and through the window saw a white car arrive. Orla and Frank. Footsteps crunched on the gravel and Mandy cried,

"Quick Harry! Throw the pills into the fire, quick! Oh Jesus..."

It Couldn't Have Happened to a Nicer Man

Sergeant Malone's eyelids closed into nutshells and he exhaled like a punctured tire when he heard a car pull into the barracks yard. *Kitty Kelly, the new constable.* No sooner had he conjured up her name than she was standing before him, right hand raised in salute.

"Kitty Kelly, skipper," she announced. Malone looked at her with weary eyes. She was a big woman, six foot four and almost two hundred pounds weight, he reckoned. They shook hands.

"Sit down Kitty," he said, "welcome to Bearnagweithe."

"Glad to be here," she replied, looking around for a chair, "Who's that fella in the red ski suit I saw downtown?"

"Red ski suit? Oh, that's Spoke Whelan, he's harmless."

"What's his game?" Kitty quizzed, taking off her cap.

"Resident genius," said the sergeant, looking at her hair, bottle blonde and cropped nearly to the bone. Oh Jesus, he thought, they've sent me the Gestapo. Sergeant Malone opened a manila folder and yawned, "I've booked you into the Imperial Hotel until you find a place of your own…"

"Fine. What kind of a patch have you here?"

"It's quiet, as a rule…"

Constable Kitty Kelly drove slowly to the Imperial Hotel, checking out the town. She saw the oddball in the red ski suit again and stared at him until he hurried down a laneway. She wondered about the nun-like waif with the quick walk, and circled the Square to get a better glimpse of her face. "This place is full of weirdoes," Kitty thought, nosing into a parking spot in front of the hotel.

She was just about satisfied with her room, which had a view of the town Square and a rusty wrought iron balcony. The bed was large with a good mattress and the wardrobe had plenty space for all her luggage and boxes of baggage.

Kitty looked out the window and scanned the town. It was no great shakes: hodge-podge shops and houses, badly parked cars and no people to be seen apart from the lady stepping out of the bank across the Square. The policewoman watched her, a redhead with a confident walk. Good legs, thought Kitty, stepping back from the window as the lady approached the hotel.

When Constable Kelly entered the dining room, the redhead was sitting alone at a table by the window. Engrossed in her newspaper, she was startled when the policewoman asked,

"Mind if I join you?"

"No, no. Please do," she replied to the woman in blue uniform.

"Thanks. Kitty Kelly, latest addition to the forces of law and order here."

"Oh! I'm Joan Long, I work at the bank."

They made small talk. Kitty quizzed Joan about the town social life, flats, and such. She smiled into the bank teller's innocent brown eyes, gazed at her neck and looked lovingly at her slender hands. A virgin, she thought, noticing no rings on the fingers, no sorrow in the soul.

Kitty' was enjoying her main course until a man came to the table in a whirlwind of greetings.

"Hello, hello, hello!" announced Malcolm Finn, pulling out a chair and joining them. Joan greeted him and Kitty stared at the intruder.

"It's good manners to ask if you may sit," she said coldly.

"I beg your pardon?" stammered Malcolm, ruddy as a beetroot, "this is my table, and I always dine here."

Joan got flustered, wiped her mouth with a napkin and apologized that the confusion was her fault; she should have informed Constable Kelly that it was Malcolm's regular table. Kitty grunted and stabbed a roast potato with her fork, speckling gravy on the tablecloth. Malcolm bit his lip, put on his spectacles and stared blankly at the menu. He felt uncomfortable, face boiling, mist of sweat on his brow. Kitty eyed him sullenly: a soft man in late midlife, dressed impeccably in country tweed jacket, checked shirt and bow tie. Gentry, she thought, chewing a lump of steak.

Malcolm ordered a schooner of sherry to start with, baked haddock to follow, easy on the white sauce, plenty broccoli and hold the carrots. Joan asked how his orchids were coming along and he sipped his sherry and said,

"Very well actually. Last week's sun did them a barrel of good so they're just on the verge of opening...that's the most exciting time...just when..."

"So where would you advice me to start looking for a flat?" Kitty cut in, addressing herself to Joan.

"Ah...well I got mine through the local newspaper, *The Independent.*"

"How big is your place?"

"Just a studio really, bedroom off a living-room cum kitchen. But tiny all the same...I've been trying to persuade Malcolm here to rent me part of his place but he won't budge."

Malcolm smiled uneasily.

"The old servants quarters, you know...disused and in a terrible state...not rentable in it's present state right now..."

"I wasn't asking." Kitty stopped.

"I'm sorry, please excuse me ladies." Malcolm said and drained his sherry. He rose from the table and left the dining room with a proud walk.

"Who's that weirdo?" asked Kitty.

"Malcolm Finn," sighed the bank teller as she rooted in her handbag for anxiety pills, "A gentleman farmer who lives a mile or so outside the town. He's very well off but a little eccentric...a bachelor who won't ever marry."

"Who'd want to marry a sponge like him?"

"Ah he's a nice man though, it just takes a while to get to know him. He hasn't much else apart from the flowers...anyway I'd better get back to work. It was nice meeting you Kitty, and welcome to town."

"Thanks. And listen, I'll see you around. We might meet for a drink or something. I'm staying here in the hotel."

It rained on and off for the next week and Kitty prowled around the town, shoulders back, eyes searching, intense as a spotlight. One day she cautioned two town deadbeats for loitering around the public toilets in the Square. Another time she asked Jake Sloecome if he had permission to display a sandwich sign on the footpath outside his bookshop. On market day, she followed Spoke Whelan for two hours, as he slowly walked every street, alley and lane in the town, eyes to the ground, looking for a diamond he had seen in a dream. She knocked off the surveillance when he bowed into St. Colman's church for inspiration.

Off duty, Kitty took to the bed and fantasized about Joan Lyons. But she didn't join her for lunch again, sat alone instead at a round table in the dining room and brooded while Joan and Malcolm Finn joked at his spot by the window.

One evening, just as dusk fell and rain pelted in squalls, Kitty snared Joan as she left the bank. They walked briskly to the teller's flat and Kitty whispered, "Would there be any chance of a cup of tea? I'm perished with the cold."

"Sure," said Joan, opening the door, "come in. Sorry that the place is in a mess..."

"It's fine," Kitty replied.

The first thing the policewoman noticed was the underwear drying on the back of a chair by the fireplace and her blood heated up. Joan brought tea and biscuits on a tray and whipped the undies away in embarrassment.

"They shouldn't be there," she said in a half-laugh.

"What's natural is wonderful," Kitty chuckled.

They sipped tea and complained about the weather and the lack of life in the town. Kitty smiled and said, "We should go away some weekend—hit the hot spots in Dublin..."

"Yeah," Joan said dreamily, "actually I haven't been in Dublin for ages..."

"What about going there some weekend?" Kitty pressed.

"Yeah, maybe. It's a thought. Would you like more tea or another biscuit?"

"Yes please. And by the way, I love your hair. Beautiful cut."

"Really? Do you think so Kitty?"

After that evening, Kitty regularly called on Joan for late afternoon tea and biscuits. She subtly tried to woo the banker away from Malcolm Finn's table and was surprised when Joan said,

"Actually Kitty, in an odd sort of a way I feel that Malcolm needs me. He likes the company and loves discussing girly things ...you know...like he loves talking about perfume and make-up...He's odd I suppose but the poor man is harmless."

Kitty felt like savaging Malcolm, decrying him as a fruit, an impotent wimp. But she felt that might have an undesirable effect. Instead she philosophized about sexuality and deviance in a most compassionate way.

"Different strokes for different folks," she said softly, "it takes all types to make the world.

On a late-night prowl around town, Kitty spotted Malcolm Finn driving down Clare Street and wondered where he was going. She gazed after the car as it wound slowly down the street and turned up Briar Hill. At least he's not going to see my honey, Kitty thought, fondling the undies in her pocket that she had earlier nicked out of Joan's laundry basket in the bathroom.

Undies were also on Malcolm Finn's mind that night. He parked in the shadows outside St. Mary's Church and sat in his car, listened to the wind whip the black leafless trees and frowned at wisps of cloud gliding past a crescent moon. Malcolm left the car quietly and melding with the shadows; he walked by the high churchyard wall and crossed through the cemetery, shutting out the whispers of his dead ancestors. At the end of the burial ground he stooped by an iron gate and fiddled with the lock keep. Gently he coaxed the heavy barrier open and slipped into the convent grounds.

Malcolm made his way through the high-hedged garden, which he often visited with Mother Superior. At the tall monument of the Crucifixion he veered left and turned into the drying-yard by the laundry. His mouth watered: lazily swaying in dim the moonlight, dozens of schoolgirls' underwear boggled his mind. "Ahhh!" he gasped and rushed across the cobblestone yard.

Just as Malcolm reached for a pair of black tights, he was dazzled by a blaze of lights. He shielded his eyes in fright. A bell rang somewhere and the convent wolfhound barked. Panic stricken, Malcolm ran but couldn't find a way out of the yard. He heard voices, dozens of voices and he covered his head with his jacket. The hands of ten nuns grabbed him, and he fell to the ground weeping, clutching a pair of black tights.

Mother Superior was kind to Malcolm and gave him hot cocoa with a good shot of brandy. Sitting in her office, he confessed his mission and told her about his closet life. She pursed her lips and stared at her desk while wondering if the same rules of sin applied to non-Catholics like him. He was always different, she thought, remembering their excursions to garden shows around the country. How could a man who was so passionately in love with flowers be a sinner as well? No, she concluded, Malcolm was not a sinner, he was just ill.

"Malcolm," she said quietly, "I think you should see Doctor Maura. I'll make an appointment for you and we'll forget all about this incident."

Doctor Maura knew Malcolm well; they often played bridge together, he attended her New Year's Eve party and she never missed his annual birthday bash in the manse. A kind faced woman with grey hair in a bun, she sat at her surgery desk and opened his medical file. Malcolm nervously fingered his tweed hat.

"I'm not gay," he muttered, "I just like wearing women's clothes..."

Dr. Maura nodded. "It's nothing to be ashamed of," she consoled, "you're a cross-dresser."

He made a whimpering sound and checked himself promptly, sat erect in the chair. Dr. Maura trotted out case histories and informed him that there were other closet cross-dressers in the area and he was not alone. She took off her spectacles and said,

"Once you have the clothes, you'll be fine."

It took him a couple of days to raise the subject with Joan Long. She was supping her soup when he whispered that he was a cross-dresser. Her eyes widened and the spoon halted before her mouth. Malcolm waited for the news to settle and was heartened when she said,

"I'm still your friend, your private life is your own business."

He clasped her hand and muttered.

"Thank you Joan, thank you."

At dessert he wondered if she might do him a huge favor: help him buy a couple of feminine outfits. Without hesitation Joan agreed and Malcolm closed his eyes with a sweet smile.

Kitty Kelly called on Joan that evening and they had tea and biscuits in front of the fire. The policewoman again suggested going away for the weekend; Willie Nelson was playing in Dublin and she could get tickets. Joan winced and said that she had a prior arrangement with Malcolm. Kitty's head jerked backwards.

"Joan," she sighed, "I don't know for the life of me, what you see in him."

On Saturday morning Malcolm collected Joan and they drove to Galway. A cheerful drive over the mountains, opera on the radio, she explaining the qualities of different fabric and cloth, Malcolm confiding fantasies. And you'll probably want make-up, she said, looking at his face and wondering what would suit.

Joan suggested they shop at Brown Thomas and she led him through the various departments. Malcolm was in ecstasy and admired lingerie, negligees, underwear. He swooned at mannequins and realized he needed a wig as well, brunette he thought; blonde would suit better, Joan advised. When he'd picked out what he wanted, she took the items to the counter and they carried four huge bags of goodies back to the car.

"This truly has been one of the happiest days in my life," he said as they drove home, "Thank you Joan, thank you."

Malcolm shaved his legs that night and pulled on panties and tights. Stuffed the cups of his black bra with tissues and tied it over his chest. He selected a pale satin blouse from the three he'd got and stood in front of the full-length mirror, tied the buttons, settled the collar. Then he took a brown tweed skirt from the hanger, opened the zip and stepped into it. Sat at the dressing table in his bedroom and carefully applied make-up to his face. Finally he donned the blonde wig and settled the crown on his head. Malcolm looked at his transformed reflection in the mirror and gasped, "Oohh la-la..."

He had a rapturous evening in the manse, lounged in the sitting room under paintings of his ancestors, played Mozart on the hi-fi and got tipsy on champagne. At bedtime he slowly undressed, put his clothes away neatly and pulled on a crimson negligee with black trim. Washed off the make-up, applied moisturizing cream to his face and went to bed with his blonde wig on.

"At last I'm myself," he muttered to the pillow.

At lunch the following Monday, he told Joan about his nights at home. I'd love to have seen you, she giggled and Malcolm broke into uncontrollable laughter that turned the heads of other diners. Kitty Kelly shot him a caustic look and he blushed and dabbed sweat from his forehead with a napkin.

"God Malcolm," Joan said quietly, "I have never seen you happier."

"I know," he chuckled, "I know."

Some nights later as Malcolm sipped sherry in a tight black velvet dress, he decided to pay a surprise visit on Joan. Maybe pick up the back issues of Cosmopolitan that she'd promised him. He examined his make-up, settled the wig, and sprayed a little Estee Lauder on his neck. Perfect, he smiled, posing this way and that in front of the mirror. What a surprise she'll get, he chuckled. First time ever outside the manse in woman's dress, he felt overwhelmed by freedom, looked at the black sky with outstretched hands and said,

"Thank you God, thank you for being good to Malcolm."

He was unprepared for the difficulties of driving with high heels and the car growled painfully as he changed gears. It took all the concentration he had to control the vehicle and a couple of times he thought he heard his mother's voice pleading with him to turn around and go back home. "It's the sherry," he chuckled. "Mother loved sherry."

On the outskirts of the town a figure emerged from the darkness. Malcolm saw the luminous belt and the blue uniform commanding him to stop.

"Good grief!" he muttered and halted.

Kitty Kelly peered at the vehicle registration number and then looked at the driver. Malcolm Finn in black velvet dress, blonde wig and scarlet lipstick. Her chest expanded and she towered over the car.

"Kitty," he stammered, "us ladies have to stick together."

"Get out of the car, you pervert," the policewoman ordered, fingers squeezing her black truncheon.

WAITING FOR A MIRACLE

OVER THE CLANGING AND HAMMERING OF THE BUILDING SITE, workmen heard a scream and when they went to investigate, Moscow Honan was lying on his back near a dump truck. His hard hat was by the front wheel and he howled, trying to lift himself on his elbows. Ten men or more surrounded him and a young carpenter dialed 999 on his mobile phone. Pete Mac, the foreman took control and knelt beside his fellow worker.

"Don't move Moscow," he whispered, "don't move."

More men gathered around and Pete took off his jacket, rolled it in a pillow and eased it under Moscow's head.

"What happened?" he asked quietly, "Where are you hurt?"

Moscow tried to mutter but cut into a scream.

"There's no blood," someone noted.

"His back might be broken," an old bricklayer whispered, "he looks like Johnny Fox when he fell from the crane."

An ambulance blared into the site and paramedics jumped out and went to Moscow. They took his pulse, looked into his eyes but could get no sense from him. Carefully they lifted him on a stretcher and put him into the ambulance, slammed the door shut and sped down Sea Road to the hospital. The workmen watched the flashing lights until the ambulance sped over Boherbwee Hill.

"Did anyone see what happened to him?" Pete Mac asked, but nobody had.

A site-office clerk phoned Moscow's wife with news of the incident and Pete Mac and an engineer followed the ambulance to the hospital. Moscow was in critical care unit when they got there and they sat in a bare yellow waiting room, near a small aquarium. The engineer stared at a goldfish that stared back at him and the foreman read a woman's magazine.

Mrs. Honan arrived with a neighbour and the men stood up and stammered how sorry they were for her troubles.

"Please God everything will be fine," the engineer said in a soft voice.

A nurse with a kind face came and took Moscow's wife aside.

"He's stable," she whispered, "we've sent him down to X-ray. We can't discern any injuries apart from a bruise on his left hip." The wife nodded, went back to the foreman and whimpered.

"What did you do to my Moscow?" He shook his head and

looked at the engineer.

"We found him on the ground...nobody saw what happened to him," said the engineer.

"If he's not all right, ye're in big trouble," she warned.

For days, doctors and nurses tested Moscow, X-rayed him, scanned him and computerised him. They found no injuries and yet he moaned and groaned like he was in terrible pain. He was inject-ed, given painkillers, given a drip. His wife sat beside his bed and held his hand. Flowers and cards arrived from his fellow building workers; a case of Lucozade came from the local pub and grapes from the football club. When anybody inquired of his condition, his wife shook her head and sighed,

"I'm afraid my poor Moscow will never be the same again."

He came home in a hospital wheelchair, his head slumped into his chest. When friends called, Mrs. Honan said,

"He's not able to see anyone. Say a prayer or light a candle for him. I'll let ye know when he's cheered up a bit."

Mr. Hickman, a lawyer who specialised in compensation claims, was the only one outside of family who was allowed to visit the invalid. He asked what happened and Moscow shook his head.

"I can't remember anything. I just remember being in the hospital."

The lawyer nodded. Moscow wept.

"I'm completely shagged. I can't even get up outa bed for a piss."

"You'll be grand, you'll be grand," the lawyer said.

He had read the doctors' reports; they could find nothing wrong apart from a small purple bruise on his left hip. They were puzzled as to why he was disabled.

"I think he should see an independent specialist," Mr. Hickman recommended to Moscow's wife.

The patient was taken to a private clinic in Dublin and spent a week there. The specialist could find nothing out of order and when speaking to the lawyer on the phone he said,

"It might all be in his mind."

"Does it matter where it is?" the lawyer asked, "If he can't walk, he can't walk."

After two month of letters and meetings with Mr. Hickman and specialists, Mrs. Honan said,

"Lourdes is the only hope, "maybe he'll be miraculously cured."

The building workers collected five hundred fedros and gave it to her and the V de P gave two hundred more. Moscow's old darts team held a fund-raiser; neighbours collected door to door; shop-keepers put donation boxes on their counters and enough money was gathered to send him and his wife to Lourdes for two weeks. Thirty friends and well-wishers accompanied them to Shannon Airport and Moscow feebly raised his hand in thanks before his wife wheeled him into the departures lounge.

"We'll pray for ye all," she told them with a blessing of her hands.

Moscow was brought to the baths every day and immersed in the cold water with hundreds of sick and infirm. His wife sent home blessed postcards and bought dozens of souvenirs that proclaimed "I prayed for you at Lourdes." Back home, the town waited for word of a cure. Praying hard as Moscow, they scoured newspapers and listened to the radio for news.

A crowd of supporters went to the airport to welcome the pilgrim home, hoping he'd walk through the arrivals door. Saddened by the sight of him slumped in the wheelchair, yet they clapped and cheered.

"It did him some good anyway," his wife said, "he's not as depressed as he was."

Settled back at home, Mrs. Honan doled out medals, souvenirs and bottles of holy water. When she ran short of the sacred aqua, she filled baby whiskey bottles with tap water so that no caller left empty-handed. The lawyer received a glass statue of Our Lady of Lourdes and Father Linnane got a music box that played *Ave Maria*.

"We were hoping for a miracle," she told the priest, "but it wasn't our turn."

"God is good," Fr. Linnane reminded. "He has a special place in his heart for Moscow."

Mr. Hoffman, the building contractor was served with a claim for 3 million fedros on behalf of Moscow and he raised his eyebrows and passed it on to his insurance company. Letters fluttered between lawyers and Moscow was asked to attend for medical examination. Teams of doctors and specialists examined him for days on end, but found no reason why he could not walk. The insurance company wrote back to Moscow's lawyer and firmly disputed the claim.

"Take them to court," the wife said, "if it costs me every penny I have, I'll get justice for my Moscow."

"We're all behind Moscow," Mr. Hickman said, looking her straight in the eyes. Holding his gaze like a laser light that went all the way to the back of his skull, she said, "And no foal, no fee."

That night, neighbours heard shouting and banging of doors coming from the Honan home. The following night the racket erupted again and when they heard off-key singing, a neighbour said, "That sounds like Moscow."

Others who heard the singing also thought it sounded like him. Some wondered if Lourdes had helped him and others wondered if the strain of the lawsuit had triggered his spirit. But when Mrs. Honan wheeled him up to the front of the church for Sunday Mass, he looked slumped as a scarecrow in a rumbled blue suit and tweed cap shadowing his eyes. There wasn't a stir out of him when Fr. Linnane offered up prayers for his recovery.

A holy friend of the family recommended Moscow go to Fatima and Fr. Linnane was roped into raising funds. He hinted to Mrs. Honan that maybe it was too soon to be knocking on heaven's door again, but she reminded him that God had a special place for Moscow. A man from the local radio station interviewed Mrs. Honan and a reporter for *The Champion* wrote a story about her husband. Thousands of fedros were donated and Mrs. Honan said, "If Fatima doesn't work, we'll bring Moscow to Medjugorje."

A stream of postcards flowed to the town from Fatima and pictures of Moscow at the holy shrine were printed in the local papers. There was no miracle and when they returned home Mrs. Honan announced,

"We're very disappointed, but we know that no prayer goes to waste."

Fr. Linnane heard a whisper from a priest that Moscow and his wife were spotted dancing and carousing at Club Blanc a Blanc in Fatima.

"No, Jack," he said to his informant, "it couldn't be them…it must be another couple…I know the Honans."

"I'm only passing on what I heard from the Miracle Bureau— you know how they keep track of things, just in case. They probably have photographic evidence."

"But surely it's all irrelevant…you know…I mean he wasn't cured…he's still in the wheelchair."

"As I said Tom, I'm only passing on what I heard."

Fr. Linnane came to visit and Mrs. Honan sat him by the fire and made tea. She gave him bottles of holy water, medals and a statue with a holy relic. He thanked her and asked about Fatima and their time there. Serving tea she whispered,

"Father, I'd tell this to no wan else but yourself…Moscow lost his faith in Fatima."

The priest shuddered. Heaviness enveloped the room and he found it hard to breathe.

"Good God!" he muttered after a few seconds. Mrs. Honan poured him a glass of brandy and explained.

"When there was no miracle, he gave up on God. It breaks my

heart to hearing him cursing Holy Jesus and the apostles."

"Good God," repeated the priest, "good God. Should I have a word with him?"

Mrs. Honan sighed.

"He's a bit depressed today. It wouldn't be a good time to talk to him. But d'you know what I was thinkin'?"

She looked Fr. Linnane straight in the eye and bore a tunnel into his brain that made him dizzy. He heard her say,

"If there was anything at all that you could do so he gets a good compensation, I'd say he'd come back to the rails...as far as he could. He's given up on the miracles."

"Well...I can pray...I'm always praying for a recovery."

"Maybe you could pray for both...work two miracles."

On a sunny afternoon, some weeks later, children whipped spinning tops in the town Square and two traveling musicians played fiddle and accordion at a street corner. Fr. Linnane was returning home from stroll by the river when he saw two well-groomed men in suits and tight haircuts leaving Peter McCabe's. They shook hands with Peter and the curate heard them speaking as they left him.

"And don't forget to read the literature," said one.

Seeing the priest, McCabe closed the door quickly. The men nodded to the pastor and he read the nametags on their jackets: Elder Charles Jones, Elder Samuel Hicks. Mormons. Competition. The priest slowed his pace, stopped and looked at the televisions in the window of Harney's Electric Emporium. Tens of TVs played a John Wayne movie, *The Quiet Man*. Fr. Linnane stood and watched

Wayne drink whiskey with a leprechaun. Every now and the priest glanced down the street and watched the Mormons go door to door until they turned Gallery's Corner. He winced when John Wayne got into a brawl, and moved on to the presbytery for his tea.

Mrs. Honan greeted the Mormons with a real Irish welcome and invited them inside. She seated them around the kitchen table and served tea and homemade scones. They liked the dainties so much, that she insisted they have the recipe and got a pen and wrote it out for each of them. She let them talk until they tired and then Elder Hicks asked if she had any questions. Mrs. Honan looked him in the eyes, told about Moscow and how hard it was to keep the show on the road. They sympathised and she wondered if they had any sort of charities that helped out hard cases like hers. Elder Jones opened a notebook and wrote out details; his companion gave her booklets with pictures and explained more about their church. Mrs. Honan wondered if they'd like to see Moscow and they said sure, and followed her up a narrow dark stairway. She knocked gently on his bedroom door and spoke quietly, "It's only me." Mrs. Honan turned to the Elders and whispered, "Stay here. I'll have a word with him first."

Minutes later she returned and said,

"He's a bit tired but ye can talk to him."

The drapes were closed and the room was dark and warm, with a heavy odour of take away food and cigarettes. Elder Jones coughed and Mrs. Honan muttered,

"God bless you."

Moscow was raised on pillows, blankets half up his chest. The preachers introduced themselves and he wheezed,

"Ye're welcome to Ballygale, what can I do for ye?"

"Well Sir," said Elder Hicks, "we'd like to tell you about our wonderful church..."

After a few minutes, Moscow interrupted the rap and asked,

"Have ye any hymns? Isn't it ye that have the great choir?"

"Yes sir," smiled Elder Jones, "the Tabernacle Choir, Salt Lake City, that's us."

"We saw ye on the Discovery channel," said Mrs. Honan, "we got the satellite when poor Moscow had the accident."

"Give us a hymn," encouraged Moscow.

"Do," added his wife.

"Well we don't have great voices," chuckled Elder Hicks.

"Come on now," coaxed Mrs. Honan, "all Mormons have great voices. Go on, a hymn'd cheer up poor Moscow no end."

"Go on," urged Moscow, "anything at all, *Silent Night* even."

Elder Hicks had a fit of coughing and Elder Jones said,

"This room is very stuffy. . .it's not good for your health Moscow."

"I'll open the window," Mrs. Honan said, pulling back the brown drapes and letting light into the room. Moscow shielded his eyes and swore. She swore back and let down the window to the stop.

"Now," she said, "give us *Silent Night*.

"Go on," ordered Moscow.

After a shaky start, *Silent Night* filled the room and headed out the window and up the town, to meld with fiddle and accordion music coming from Looney's pub.

"Beautiful," praised Mrs. Honan, "absolutely beautiful."

"Ye'll have to give us another wan," Moscow pleaded.

"What about *Faith of Our Father*?" wondered his wife.

"I'm afraid we don't know that one," Elder Jones said.

"Ye must know the *Adeste*," Moscow hoped. Elder Hicks coughed and Mrs. Honan handed him a glass of water from the bedside table.

"Have ye any song about that prophet ye were talkin' about?"

Elder Jones looked at his watch. His companion cautiously sipped water from Moscow's glass.

"Wan for the road," Mrs. Honan said.

"Don't rush them," her husband chided.

The Elders looked at each other.

"Maybe *Golden Gates of Heaven*?" Samuel suggested.

Crows were flocking over the town for their evening aerobatics when the Salt Lake preachers left Honan's and Cissy Goggins calculated they had been there for nearly three hours. She told Fr. Linnane the following day at confessions, but he knew already. On Sunday, Mrs. Honan went to church alone and sat up in the front pew where she used be with Moscow. When she caught the priest's eye, she shook her head sadly and he turned around and raised his hands up to heaven.

During the week she met Fr. Linnane on the street and urged him to prayer harder, because a court date had been set to hear Moscow's compo claim. Judgment day was nigh. The priest asked how Moscow was bearing up and she said, "Wan day good and another day bad."

He didn't mention the Mormons.

On the countdown to the court date, different Mormons visited Moscow. They always sang for him and said they were there to give the Honans strength. Elder Hicks often came with Elder Bates, and Elder Shultz sometimes accompanied Elder O'Brien. Moscow liked Elder O'Brien, an Irish-American who answered the bedridden man's queries on polygamy. Moscow followed up his train of thought with Elders Hicks and Bates, but they were less forthcoming.

One evening Shultz mentioned to Mrs. Honan that Moscow might be drinking and she inhaled sharply and whispered,

"He's goin' on the dry when this is all over."

Ernest Shultz smiled and said affectionately,

"Moscow's a good man, and he's got a great woman."

"I get a bit worried when he talks about the polygimmick thing."

"There's very little polygamy Ma'am, only in remote areas."

"We're remote enough around here."

The week before the court case, a choir of Mormons came twice, and almost every night neighbours heard drunken singing, regular arguments and wall thumping coming from Moscow's house. One night they heard Mrs. Honan shout.

"Only for me you'd be still drivin' nails for Hoffman."

Moscow's reply was slurred but audible:

"I should have left you in the shit house with Farley."

Court day was like an American movie, with all the sleek shiny cars, and strangers in dark suits zipping up and down the stone steps of the Hall of Justice. A couple of photographers skulked around limestone columns and a mini bus of Mormons sang hymns on the lawn. Townspeople gawked at the spectacle. Lawyers in grey wigs and bat-wing cloaks flew in and out through doors and Mr. Hickman pulled nervously at the hem of his waist-coat. He looked down Parliament Street and saw Moscow's entourage approaching.

A burly youth with a shaved head and a white medical coat pushed the wheelchair. Mrs. Honan walked beside her husband, linked by a sister home from England. The medical aide was her lover. Behind them walked Mrs. Honan's two brothers, in Manchester United tracksuits, a peroxide blonde lady in fur waistcoat and bare midriff, between them.

Moscow's head was slumped forward and he looked fragile as a fledgling, fallen from a nest. His approach caused a flurry of whispers and then tense silence. Hickman trotted down the steps to greet his client and cameras began clicking and whirring. Hickman whispered that the insurance company was willing to settle for 100K. "Tell 'em to stick it," Mrs. Honan muttered and he trotted back up the steps, where lawyers looped around him.

Mr. Hickman twitched anxiously as Moscow was pushed up a special timber ramp that covered the stone steps of the courthouse. The lawyer advised Mrs. Honan that the offer had increased to 120K. Shaking her head, she continued walking towards the door of the Court No 1. Before she reached it, Hickman was back with a better offer: 150K.

"My Moscow is worth more than that," she said in a hurt voice.

"Take it," he pleaded, "there's no evidence that there's anything wrong with Moscow..."

"Moscow's fucked, man," one of her brothers said.

"We'll all be fucked if we don't settle," Hickman muttered.

"200K," Moscow whispered.

"Shut up," his wife elbowed.

"Stay there a minute," Hickman ordered and hurried back to his team.

Mrs. Honan's sister passed around chewing gum. Elder Hicks and Shultz joined them. They tapped Moscow on the shoulder and Shultz prayed,

"Moscow, may all your trials soon be over,"

"Amen," Mrs. Honan's family answered, in harmony.

Hickman came back and whispered in her ear,

"Get these people out of here..."

"They're Moscow's friends..."

"Get them out of here...Judge Rainman's wife ran away with them...Final offer 180K..."

"I'll take it Moscow," pleaded, "tell 'em I'll settle."

"Could you squeeze another 20K out of them?" Mrs. Honan asked.

"Not a chance...take it."

"I told you I'll take the fuckin' thing," Moscow hissed.

"I'll be back," Hickman said and returned to his team for another conference.

A clerk announced that court would sit in five minutes. Moscow began having little waves of panic in his stomach, even though he had taken a few fingers of brandy and a couple of Valium for breakfast. A concoction of scents and body smells wafted around him...beer, deodorant, perfume, cologne, bacon and pudding, sweat, holy books, law books, money. His vision blurred and he toppled out of the wheelchair and hit his head against the courtroom door with a loud crack.

Mrs. Honan screamed and her sister screeched. The brothers threw the wheelchair aside and bent over him. Hickman hurried across the lobby, a flock of lawyers rustling after him. Moscow's Salt Lake friends held a protective ring around the fallen man. Hickman tried to wade through, calling an ambulance on his mobile phone. Mrs. Honan wailed and swore. Her brothers shouted and Mormons prayed zealously.

Hickman stopped talking on the phone when he saw Moscow on his feet, brushing the medical aide aside. He looked dazed and took a few steps. His wife wept and hugged her sister for comfort.

"Fuck you Moscow," she wailed, "fuck you! You were never any good for anything."

"Moscow! Lie down for fuck's sake," his brother-in-law pleaded.

"What are you talking about?" Moscow asked, "Who are you?"

"Take it easy Moscow," Elder Shultz said, "take it easy, walk slowly and trust in the Lord."

"Halleluiah!" Elders rejoiced.

"What's goin' on here?" Moscow asked, the crowd giving him space.

"You've awoken from a dream!" Elder Hicks called.

"Trust in the Lord, Moscow!" Elder O'Brien cried.

Photographers clicked as Moscow walked away from his distraught wife and in-laws. Hickman came up to him and asked,

"Moscow? Do you know me? Are you alright?"

"No on all counts. Where the hell am I?"

"You're in Ballygale…Moscow, Moscow, listen to me."

"Where the hell is Ballygale? And why are you calling me Moscow? My name is Jack Lennon. I'm supposed to be getting married today but I seem to have turned up at the wrong courthouse with a crowd of lunatics."

He trotted down the courthouse steps, agile as a goat, and Elder Shultz cheered, "Praise the Lord, Moscow!" Lawyers jotted down notes and took pictures of the fleeing man with their mobile phones.

"Fuck you, Moscow!" his wife swore, "you were always a fucking idiot!"

Mr. Jones

He'll never stop drinking now. Do you think he will? I don't, he's too old to stop, he's 72. I'm 69. I probably should have left him years ago, when I was younger. But women didn't do that then, now they're gone at the drop of a hat. It's true for me. You read about them every day in the papers. Would you like a cigarette? You don't smoke? Sorry. I like the odd one myself. He smokes all the time, smoking and drinking. Of course he tried to give it up…the drinking, not the fags. He was away, you know. St. John of Gods. And St. Pats too. And of course the local place as well, he was there several times. Other institutions too, but they couldn't cure him. He didn't want to be cured, you see. My brother brought him to a special hospital in England once, very posh place. All the hob-nobs went there, but he only stayed three days. He went out a window. They called here in a panic and told me. There was nothing I could do. Eventually the police found him drinking with winos in Nottingham.

He's a disgrace. I shouldn't have married him but I knew no better then. My father thought he was a great match for me. It was my father who introduced us, you know, at the Listowel Races. I'll never forget it. You see, my father knew him from the rugby. He was a very good rugby player when he was young and they expected great things of him. Thought he'd play for Ireland. Of course he didn't. Couldn't even make the Connaught team. The drink. After we married he said we'd build a house outside the town. I was looking forward to that. We were going to have a family then. But none of that ever happened.

We were living here with his mother, you see. She adored him and she didn't like me. She was always sighing around me. Terrible. She was a right old battle-axe. He couldn't stand her either. And of course that was a great excuse to be away drinking, instead of building our own house, up in the land. You know? I was looking after the business and looking after her. It wasn't easy. For God's sake, who ever saw a woman butcher? I was a nurse one minute and the next I was selling sausages. But I had to do it. He wasn't here.

That time he had a contract to supply meat to the girls' boarding school, St Ita's up the road. Many's the time the nuns had to come down here and ask where was their meat. He'd have forgotten to deliver it. Might not even have prepared their order. I used be mortified. I used go to all the pubs around town looking for him. If I found him, he often wouldn't leave and even told me to eff off a few times. Terrible. I should have left him then. But instead I tried to keep the show on the road. The nuns went elsewhere for their meat for a finish. You couldn't blame them. Can you imagine, two hundred students waiting for their dinner and the butcher refusing to give them meat? It was terrible.

Of course it got worse when his mother died. An excuse, that's all it was. He didn't love her. I knew that, he told me often. He never loved anybody but the drink, and the fags. And he was a fine-looking fellow, you know, rugged and handsome. A lot of rugby players are, aren't they? And he was very strong, only for that, the drink would have killed him. I don't know how he isn't dead. You know he has a plate in his skull? A steel plate, the result of a car crash. He went over the wall one night coming home from Galway and the car tumbled into a quarry. They found him in the morning. He was brought to Dublin. He was anointed that time. They thought he was going to die, but he surprised them. I thought that would stop the drinking but it didn't. He was back on it a few months afterwards. He's incurable.

Another time he drove into a lorry in broad daylight up the street. The fire brigade had to cut him out and he broke a leg and an arm. But he still didn't learn. I don't know why, because he's an intelligent man, isn't he? Do you think so? I do. And he had a great education, Rockwell College. He was a few years at university studying medicine, but he didn't mind the books and spent his time playing rugby. That's how my father knew him, the rugby. My father was chairman of Blackhall Rugby Club. My father could see no wrong in him, but my mother could, and was wary of him. She was right. I didn't see it her way, you don't when you're young, sure you don't?

He'll outlive me. I know that. He's strong. One night, he came back and I was in bed. I didn't hear him coming in. He went to the bathroom and fell into the bath, on his back. And I had clothes steeping in the bath in bleach. And he fell asleep with water up to his ears. Never woke up until I found him in the morning. I screamed when I saw him. I though he was dead. You would, wouldn't you, when you'd see someone like that lying in the bath of water like a corpse. He effed me out of it. That's what he did. And the bleach had whitened the hair at the back of his head. But out of spite, I didn't tell him. And he was going around like a fool for days...like a Frisian bull, black and white. It was good enough for him.

He's proud, you know. That's the breeding. The father's side. Big shots in a small town. Often he'd look at the name over the shop and walk around the front of the place like it was a castle. That was when he did a bit of butchering. But I think he felt it was beneath him somehow and he spent less and less time here. Always had other things to do, and there was always drinking to be done. You know, racing and rugby and the Spring Show in Dublin. And of course the Fianna Fail Ard Fheis, that was a big one. Lots of big talk, and loads of brandy, slipping and slobbering in hotels until daylight. Fairs, he couldn't miss any sort of a fair either, Spancil Hill, Ballinasloe, the Puck Fair, horse fairs, antique fairs. Anything. All dressed up like a lord. He was always gone. Wherever there was a racket, he was there.

For a finish he didn't butcher any meat. Didn't cut anything, just ordered it in from some place in Galway. It came in brown cardboard boxes, you know—chickens and sausages, chops, puddings, bacon and that sort of thing. He'd just put it out on trays and leave me to sell it. Of course I was more of the fool to do it. You can be a fool in marriage, can't you? It took me years to find that out. Are you married? No? And have you a girlfriend. You do? That's good. I'd say you're good to her, you've that look about you.

Do you know his brother? The canon? Lovely man. They don't talk at all. Haven't for years. They had a row, up at the hotel one evening. It was terrible. The bishop and all the priests of the diocese were there. I think it was after Confirmation, yes, yes it was. And he came in and gate-crashed their gathering, you know, barged into the room where they were having a quiet drink or whatever. The canon told me came about it later. You see, the canon knew he was drunk and tried to wheel him out before any trouble started, but he wasn't able. Then they had a row. The canon was mortified because my fellow shouted that the bishop was having an affair with a certain nun. Maybe he was, I don't know. The hotel people called the guards and he was arrested. He refused to apologise to the bishop. Only for that, the canon would be a monsignor, maybe even a bishop now. But that finished him. After that the poor man was transferred to a parish in the back of beyond. They haven't spoken since.

Of course that wasn't the first time he was arrested, oh God no, he has been arrested several times. And always got away with it. Connections, you see, since his rugby days. If right was right he should have gotten jail a few times. But he didn't. There's no justice, is there? It all depends on who you know. One time he was arrested for striking a publican up the town. He broke his jaw because the man refused to serve him. He was drunk, very drunk. I think it was after a funeral or something. He loves funerals. Sometimes I think he only gets up out of bed to go to funerals. The first thing he does in the morning is to read the death notices in the newspapers. That isn't normal, is it? So he broke that poor man's jaw and was arrested in another pub down the street. He was singing a song apparently when the guards came in for him and he wouldn't leave until the song was finished. They brought him to court and the judge just bound him to the peace for two years. Terrible wasn't it? After breaking a poor man's jaw. He said he didn't mean it, that it was a friendly tap. Friendly tap! I heard the courtroom was in stitches. He should have got jail, but you see he had the connections.

And when I think of all the times he was pulled for drunken driving. And got away scot free mostly. Except for the time he was caught in the North somewhere. Ballymena I think. He was up at a rugby match and of course was drinking his way home. It was the army who stopped him and he became very abusive apparently, told them he'd get the IRA after them. Can you imagine? Nobody in their right mind would say a thing like that. Sure they wouldn't? But he did. So they arrested him, and rightly so. He was locked up for days. The guards came here to the door at three in the morning to tell me. I thought he was dead when I heard the knock.

They let him out on bail, I can't remember what it was but it was a lot of money at the time, several thousand pounds anyway. And then he had to go to court up there, which was a different kettle of fish than going before one of his cronies down here. Oh it was in the papers and all. The judge called him a disrespectful thug who shouldn't drink. He gave him a big lecture and a huge fine and would have put him in jail were it not for pressure from the

Taoiseach. He knew the Taoiseach from the rugby, you see, and the Ard Fheises. Connections again. But of course he hated the publicity the case brought him. It was even on the radio about him. I said nothing to him. What was the point? I'd said it all already and he never listened to me anyway. "Shut up woman! Shut up woman!" is all he ever said to me.

And when he's drinking he gets into all sorts of silly business. You've seen him drinking? Haven't you? He does stupid things and gets into terrible messes. Like that time himself and that…oh what's his name…the fella from Mayo…I can't think of him now…but anyway, they stole cattle one night over in Offaly. Total madness. They were after bringing over two horses to some trainer there and of course there was drink involved. So they stole cattle from a farm near Portumna and brought them home in the lorry. Worse, the fools put them into our fields. He was in court for that too but got away with it. And when you'd see him in the morning after he gets up, and he dressed like Prince Phillip, you'd swear he was a proper gentleman, wouldn't you. He dresses well, I have to say that for him. That's the best I can say about him.

He goes to Cheltenham every year, you know, for the races. Once he was away for nearly three weeks. He had a big win, that's what he told me on the phone. I could hear a party going on in his room, women laughing and somebody singing. I hung up on him. The next day I closed the butcher shop, why should I slave and he having a good time? And I always wanted to have a shoe shop so I got Tommy Hynes the builder to come in and change everything, take out the big cold room and the display cases and all that kind of thing. My brother has a fine shoe shop in Kilkenny and he supplied me with stock to get it started. I should have done it years before, but you don't think of the obvious sometimes, sure you don't? When he came back from Cheltenham he was so drunk that he didn't even notice the change in the place. It was a week or more before he realised it.

One morning he went out to the shop in his striped butchers' apron and stood behind the counter. Big man trying to make an impression, you know? He'd do that sometimes, pretend to me he was turning over a new leaf, especially if he'd overdone something. Atoning for his sins. Lot of sighing, like his mother. And standing at the door, smoking and chit-chatting. But he was too sick to go to the door this morning and he just stood behind the counter. I was watching him from the kitchen. He looked around the shop, and all he saw were shoes. I could see the confused look on his face. He must have thought he was in the dt's because he ran upstairs to bed. We never spoke about it. I don't give him any money from the shop. Why should I? His father left him a millionaire. He'll never drink it. Maybe that's the problem. What do you think?

Morning Tea

She woke earlier than usual, suddenly alert, like she'd parachuted into the dawn from a dreamless sleep. It was 7.15 on the digital bedside clock, and grey slivers of light crept through the sides of the curtains. She'd snooze for another hour, until Jack brought her morning cup of tea. And then it struck her that she'd talk to him today. She'd break the ice and say,

"Thanks, Jack."

Maybe she'd ask, "What kind of a day is it?" The freeze had gone on too long—two months, maybe more. She'd relent and speak to him today.

Mona turned towards the wall and pulled the duvet over her head and shoulders like a hood. The bedroom was cold, and she made a mental note to ask Jack to reset the boiler for quickening winter. She'd say it in a soft voice, maybe at teatime. They should be cautiously talking by then. She'd prepare something nice for him—one of his favourite dishes, something from their early years. Toad-in-the-Hole, Cornish Pasties, Welsh rarebit. And lunch too. When he'd come at 1pm from his job in Carney's Medical Hall, she'd have a hearty plate on the table instead of a sliced loaf and a hard lump of orange cheddar. Of course, if right was right, he should be having his lunch in Carney's. If right was right, Carney's should be theirs: she was Carney, it had been her father's business. The thought made her restless and she turned on her back and felt colder. It was Jack's fault. Her father didn't like him, thought him a wimp. And rather than pass on the business to them, he sold it instead. She didn't even get the money, her father left it all to the Vincent de Paul. That caused the first major row between her and Jack. That row lasted nearly a year and finished when she fell down the stairs and broke her ankle.

As she recovered, Jack began talking about starting a family. She'd postponed having a child while her father was alive, because the old man was adamant he'd prefer the line to be extinct than have it tainted with Jack's blood. She didn't tell this to Jack, but filed it away as ammunition for a vicious row, when she really wanted to tear out his heart. Now talk of starting a family was unnerving. She wasn't ready. The thought of coupling with Jack paled and lined her face. It slowed her recovery. One evening at tea, as he served up spicy chicken wings and French fries, he said,

"I can't wait until we're setting this table for three."

"Who's moving in?" she asked wearily.

"Well...our child...I mean not immediately...but you know what

I mean...in the future."

"Oh," she sighed, paused to push away her untouched plate and said, "If you don't mind Jack, I'd prefer not to think of that right now. I need all my energy to get on my feet again, so I don't have to depend on you."

"It's no bother to me."

"Well it bothers me Jack. And for the last month at least, it's nothing from you but having a baby, preferring a girl if it made me happier. What the hell is all this about? It's all your decision. What about me? What about me, Jack? Hmm? You lost the Medical Hall on me and now you want a baby. You're pathetic Jack."

He took his meal into the sitting room and they didn't speak again until she had to go to the hospital to have the cast removed from her leg. But he never stopped bringing her a cup of tea in the morning. That was the one constant in their marriage, Jack always brought her a cuppa in bed, and he was always waving the flag of truce. And though she despised the gesture, she always welcomed the tea.

She turned on the left shoulder and glanced at the clock: 7.40. Times goes slowly when you wake early. She'd often stayed awake right through the night, only dropping off when she heard children going to school. Many movies had run in her head in the darkness, reels of film were scattered on the floor of her mind. In some films, she was married to other men—Gabriel Byrne and Bill Clinton were husbands in a few dramas. In another feature, Jack dies, gets killed or just disappears, and she marries Robert de Niro, who's the local doctor.

The floor upstairs creaked and she perked her ears like a hound. Jack was up. More rummaging than usual. The wardrobe door creaks open, clothes hangers rattle and shoes rumble. A sneeze. Then solid footsteps across the landing and down the stairs to her floor. Right turn into the bathroom, bolts the door and water fills the hand-basin. Washing. Gurgle of wastewater. Toilet flush. Door unbolts and Jack exits the bathroom, turns left and goes down the stairs.

She waited for the snapping sound of kindling wood, waited for the scent of burning pine to weave upstairs through the thin morning air. Hearing no fire-making, she wondered what he was at. That bloody kitchen will be freezing when I get up, she thought, if he doesn't put down a fire soon. From below came the shrill whistle of the kettle on the gas burner as it boiled. At least he's making the tea, she sighed and relaxed.

Footsteps came up the stairs and she pretended to be asleep, heart pacing as she waited for Jack to twist the brass doorknob. But Jack turned right instead, and climbed the steps to the next floor. Mona opens her eyes. What's he at? Rummaging. Footsteps on the landing and down the stairs again, slowly, like he's taking one step at a time. He passes her room and descends to the kitchen. That's odd, she thought and turned on her back and looked at the ceiling.

They never had a family. After she broke the ankle, they weren't intimate again. They slept together for the warmth and security of the company, but there was no talk of babies coming into the house. She was the boss, it was her house, inherited from her grandmother.

He'd made a good catch and he should be happy to have such a sturdy roof over his head. In fairness, he wasn't demanding and was always there when she needed him. When they went out to dine with friends or to functions at the golf club or the hotel, he was the perfect partner and great company. He blossomed when they socialized with Doctor Logan and his wife, the Carters, the Faheys, or other town gentry. After Jack had a few gins, she could almost love him. It was then she saw the man she married. The vision never lasted long and the more she drank, the more he morphed into a toad. If it wasn't her house, she'd have left him years ago. She tried to throw him out several times, but he refused to go. Ignored her and went about his life as normal.

A few years after her father died, they attended a marriage counselor in Limerick. It was expensive and they went twice a month on Thursday afternoons, when the Medical Hall closed for the half-day. She remembered the journeys were long and grey, she drove her father's old Morris Oxford, because Jack never learned to drive. But he paid for the session and bought the petrol. On the way home, they stopped at the West County Grill and he was always chatty and ordered the best courses on the menu. He always said they were making progress and urged her to do the communication exercises that the counselor suggested. She promised to do them the following day but that day never came. And then, as they were about to attend their first session of the New Year, something snapped in Mona.

"This is going nowhere, Jack," she said. "I'm not wasting any-more time. This therapy thing isn't working for me."

"Just give it a few more tries, we're making progress Mona, we really are. We had the best Christmas we've ever had."

She shook her head.

"If you want, go by yourself, you can have my car."

He called the counselor and apologized that they wouldn't be making the appointment. Then wrote a check for the fees and put it in the mail.

She heard the toaster pop and then got the whiff of charred bread. Soon he'll bring the tea, she thought, maybe he was making toast for her. Maybe he'd go the extra mile and bring a glass of orange juice as well, he used do that when they were first married. Sometimes he brought her grapefruit, sprinkled with brown sugar and caramelized under the grill.

The sun came over the houses and weakly lit the room with a slice of light through the window drapes. A magpie chattered somewhere outside, and a few cars passed on their way to Ennis. The garbage truck trundled down Main Street and a school bus pulled up in the square and unloaded students. She glanced at the clock: 8.50. Christ! Where was her tea? Here he comes—the solid footstep climbing steadily, balancing the cup. A rush of thoughts scrambled through her head. What would she say to him? Thanks? Eyes open, she lay on her back, staring at the ceiling as the doorknob turned and he entered.

"You're awake," he said softly as he bent down to leave the cup and saucer on the bedside locker, "here's your tea."

She got a whiff of cologne, but said nothing, thinking he never wears cologne going to work. She decided to ignore him.

"No word today either," he said.

Jack stood beside the bed and Mona stared blankly at the ceiling. He turned away after a short while, left the room and quietly closed the door. His cologne hung in the room and she sat up in annoyance. She heard him sob quietly as he descended to the kitchen. The old softy, she sighed, what a bloody weeping willow. It's me who has cause to weep, not him. She sipped the tea: it was too strong and she angrily left it back on the locker. He can't even make a proper cup of tea anymore.

The cathedral bells pealed for morning Mass, as a car pulled up outside and someone got out. Gentle knock on the door. That's odd, she thought and wondered who it was. She felt tempted to peep out the window. The door opened and she heard the mumble of voices. A woman talking to Jack? She heard the front door close with a firm bang, car doors shut and the vehicle moved away. What was that about? Who was that woman? Did Jack go off in the car with her? Was she giving him a ride to work?

Peeved, she bounded from the bed, donned dressing gown and slippers and hurried downstairs. A sense of emptiness met her step by step and by the time she reached the ground floor, her heart was alarmed. She flashed her eyes around the kitchen, trying to understand what was different, what was wrong. Nothing was out of place, except the bunch of keys on the bare table. Jack's keys. The key of her house, the keys of Carney's Medical Hall, the key of his bicycle lock. She picked them up and hurried back upstairs, wondering where to hide them. "Such a fool," she mulled, "to leave the house without his keys."

She put them at the bottom of her underwear drawer and got back into bed to wait for his knock on the door or his call on the phone. Of course she wouldn't answer either. Rain pattered against the window and cold crept around her. Mona wondered why he hadn't put down the fire.

"What about me, Jack?" she asked the empty house, "what about me?"

FINITO

HORACE STEINER'S THERAPY ROOM WAS WARM AND SMELLED musty, with a faint whiff of heating oil. His patient, Larry Ryan, lay on the couch sobbing and Dr. Horace let him be, inhaled deeply and gazed out the window that overlooked High Street. He frowned blankly at the shoe shop on the opposite side and wondered what fantasies and troubles his next patient, Mary Kelly, would bring. After Mary's session, he'd have lunch in the Cuckoo's Nest on the quays. Today was Friday and they'd have crab cakes on the menu. He'd have those, French fries, tossed salad and a glass of wine. Maybe two glasses of wine.

Horace was past retiring age, but reluctant to give up his practice. There were a number of reasons for this. First, he didn't know what he would do with his spare time, he hadn't any hobbies or interests; once he did—stamp collecting, bird watching, a spot of polo when he was younger, golf every so often. But he'd lost interest in all of that stuff now. Second, he dreaded being at home all day with his wife, his third wife, Mary Lou. He sighed and wondered if he needed therapy himself: three wives in thirty years, not a record by a long shot. Larry King had eight, or was it nine? Could he manage a fourth wife? Mary Kelly flickered through his mind and he flexed his shoulders. No, not Mary Kelly, not another Mary.

Larry moaned and stammered an incoherent sentence. Horace turned his head away from the window, and exhaled quietly.

"That's the saddest story I've ever heard in my entire career. She took you for 200k, shot your dog and ran off with your mother's hairdresser. That's awful, really awful."

Larry wailed and curled into the fetal position.

"Horrible," Horace said, "really horrible, no wonder you're in such a state."

He left his chair and went to the cluttered desk in the corner and searched for something. Pills. He took up this bottle and that, read labels, cast them aside. Picked up another, discarded it, then another. Finally he found the correct container, Zibrax. He put two pills in a glass and filled it with water from the cooler. The water fizzed and turned green. Horace shuffled to the couch and said, "Here, this will help you."

Larry took the medicine and Horace advised him to lay still, inhale deeply and watch his breath. Horace put a tape into his boom box and played new age flute music, then lit a stick of incense.

Back in his chair, the shrink glanced around the therapy room. It was in a mess but he hadn't the interest to tidy it. If he were charging top dollar for consultations, he'd hire a cleaner. But the Irish wouldn't pay top dollar for therapy. The Irish didn't understand they had to pay someone to listen to them and try and unravel their messes and tangles. They confused him, and he could never figure if they were really telling him how things actually were with them, or if they were making it all up. Like Mary Kelly, for instance. Was she really having an affair with a priest? And did they really go to Amsterdam every month to S&M parties? He didn't know what to believe. The Irish had very fertile imaginations.

Larry was moaning again, the medicine wasn't doing the job. Horace glanced at him, pathetic clothes hanger in a crumpled suit. Larry was an engineer, worked in an office across town. Sad story, if one could believe him. Now he was bawling and stammering nonsensically.

"Take it easy," Horace said quietly, "take it easy Larry."

The phone on the desk rang and Larry powered down. The answering machine clicked in: Horace's wife Mary Lou cried 'Don't forget to get milk.' Larry sobbed again and Horace moved near him.

"Ok Larry, ok…now, here's what I want you to do…I want you to raise your left leg off the couch, as high as you can. And then, with as much force as you can muster up, slam it on the couch and shout 'I'm angry and upset but I'm ok.' Do that five times with the left leg and then do it with the right leg."

Larry did what he was told and Horace returned to his chair and stared out the window. He wondered if Larry's girlfriend really shot the dog. Shot the critter with Larry's duck hunting gun. Freud would say she was shooting Larry by proxy. Of course Freud also said the Irish were the only race in the world that couldn't be psychoanalyzed. Admittedly Freud was wrong about a number of things, but maybe he was on target about the Irish. And then it struck Horace that if he retired, he might write a book about his years giving therapy to the Irish. There was plenty of material. Subversive ballerinas, Buddhist butchers, film star typists, lesbian nuns and gay jockeys. If he had known Ireland was so weird, he'd never have left America. He should have researched the move more thoroughly. The countryside enchanted him and he was in love with Mary Lou back then and everything looked rosy, even the grey Burren hills. They came over for a tryst weekend from New York and fell in love with the place. His mind rambled back to that weekend, arriving in Shannon, driving up the coast, smoked salmon in Lisdoonvarna and an afternoon shag on the deserted beach at Bishop's Quarter.

He forgot about his patient until Larry kicked the wall with a thunderous bang that jolted Horace. Larry was in a frenzy, legs and arms flaying and thumping. Horace was taken aback. Larry jumped off the couch and attacked a filing cabinet.

"Whoa!!" Horace shouted, "Whoa, Larry…take it easy man… calm down!"

But Larry was 'out there,' tearing around the room, battering furniture, shouting.

"I'm angry and fed-up and fucked-up and nobody gives a shit and you just take my fuckin' money and buy milk for your fuckin' wife…"

"It's ok, Larry…it's ok."

"It's not fuckin' ok!!"

Larry lifted the couch with the ease of a circus strongman and flung it at Horace. It clipped the analyst who fell on the floor with a scream. The phone rang again and Larry picked it up. It was Mary Lou with another reminder about the milk.

"There will be no milk today," Larry panted, "because the cow jumped over the moon and I'm fucked if I'm goin' to run after her…I've done enough running in my life…I've had it…finito."

The door banged and Larry rattled down the stairs.

"Finito," moaned Horace, "I've had it too. I've had it with the Irish…Freud was right…they're too much for us, too much. They'll kill us before we cure them…"